MIDNIGHT HAGS

C P HOFF

ILLUSTRATED BY
MICHELLE FROESE

THE HAPPY VALLEY CHRONICLES

BOOK THREE

Adrienne
Without you there would be no Celia

To my buddy, Chen. Thanks for all the hours together sketching, colouring and encouraging. Here's to many more. M.F.

BOOKS BY CP HOFF

1

Nan cleared her throat before licking her forefinger. I almost squealed. This was the best time of day. As of late, Nan had doubled our reading time. And all because my best friend, Archibald Quigley, had thrown me over for Eugenia Whitford, the niece of my number one nemesis, Mrs. Whitford. Enid Whitford was not only the pharmacist's wife and my nan's employer; she was also a founding member of The Ladies of the Perpetual Indigence Society. Those PIS ladies—an association with the most regrettable acronym—had it in for my nan, and under the watchful eye of Mrs. Whitford mocked her at every opportunity. They'd dismiss Nan entirely, if she ever acknowledged them long enough to give them a chance. She didn't. And now Eugenia, the pissy niece of that despicable woman, had barged uninvited into my life and stolen my best friend.

All through first grade Archibald and me—yes, I know it's Archibald and *I*, but that's just too formal considering the warmth of our friendship—merrily bumped along, holding hands and swinging arms. We were as snug as two bugs in a rug. We did all the things normal friends do: dredged mud puddles for waterlogged earthworms, Frankenstein-walked at dawn, and played Jane Eyre when we were out on a stroll. (I was Jane, *obviously,* and Archibald the sickly Helen. Helen was a better match for Archibald's pallid complexion.) But then, at the start of Grade Two, in stepped Eugenia Whitford, and I was unceremoniously tossed on the refuse pile of humanity, right beside Timmy Crybaby-Head.

Cleaved from my bosom buddy at the dawn of second grade, I witnessed the remnants of my friendship with Archibald dashed upon the dusty chalkboard of an inadequate education. It wasn't just Archibald I'd been separated from; it was her entire family. Not to mention the magnificent doors to her family's library, with their carved wooden panels and brass door knockers in the shape of hands holding apples. Just thinking about it made my breath catch. But worst of all, I wouldn't be able to marvel at her magnificent mantel clock, the greatest treasure of all Happy Valley. The one Archibald's last dad ordered for her mom, hoping it would stretch out their days together. But alas, it was for naught. His days were as pinched as those of all the other husbands who came before him. Now he's dead and buried, with the rest of that unlucky crew, in the Happy Valley Graveyard, three graves down from Archibald's original dad.

My lip quivered at the thought of them. All those cold bodies lying side by side, each one dying in his own peculiar way, leaving poor Lacey—whatever her last name was at the time—to give birth to another fatherless child. It was why Archibald carried her father's given name, a living tribute to a man who would never see her face.

To comfort myself, I closed my eyes and envisioned that Prague Clock—the clock that was supposed to change every-thing. Its face was flanked by the characters of Miser, holding a bag of gold; Vanity, holding a mirror, and Worldly Pleasure, playing a lute. Last but not least was the skeleton—Death—that held an hourglass in one hand and a bell in the other. The bell rang at the top of the hour. The sound pealed through the air, telling Miser, Vanity and Worldly Pleasure that their time was up. In unison, the three amigos would shake their heads no, as if this would stave off the inevitable. I still shake my head whenever I think a clock might be chiming somewhere, just in case those three delinquents know something I don't.

The thought of Eugenia touching the brass door knocker, and breathing the air of unread books, while she listened to Archibald recite her little clock spiel—the one she'd memorized from the World Book Encyclopedia—cut me to the quick.

In my mind, unevolved Eugenia would yawn and roll her eyes. *That's nothing*, she'd say, interrupting Archibald. *We have a better clock at home. My dad ordered it from the Simpson-Sears catalogue. It has the cutest little bird that comes out, flaps its tiny wings, and tweets. Not some stupid old men wrapped up in bedsheets. They look like hippies.*

I squeezed the girls from my thoughts and turned back to Nan. She was going on and on about something I wasn't paying attention to. I smiled and nodded, letting her know I believed in her, and that what she was spouting probably had some merit. When she was satisfied she'd made her point, she opened the cover of our next adventure.

Nan didn't read me regular kid books, like *Charlie and the Chocolate Factory* or *The Giving Tree*. In fact, when the school librarian sent home *The Giving Tree*, with a note saying she hoped I'd find it inspiring, Nan was livid. She flipped through the book, grunting on almost every page. "I don't want you reading this," she said.

"Why not?"

She slapped the book shut. "Have I taught you nothing? All

the reading and prodding. Your endless interruptions and questions?"

I shrugged.

Nan groaned through her indignation. "Did you really look at what this book's about? At first glance it can seem quite sweet. Unconditional love at its finest. But that's not what's happening. The tree gives and gives of itself until there is nothing left but a stump. Yet the boy doesn't notice, let alone acknowledge what he's taken. It hurts my heart, Celia. You know how many women have lived lives like that? Thinking it's the right thing to do? Letting a man whittle them down to nothing?"

I shrugged.

"Too many. And only the men that have whittled them down to nothing are remembered." The vein in her neck pulsed. "I have never sanctioned book burning, but if ever there was a book that needed to be thrown on a pyre, it's this one."

When I told the school librarian what Nan had said, her lips thinned. "When your grandmother becomes the literary maven of Happy Valley, I'll take her opinion seriously. But until then she should keep her trap shut." She tossed *The Giving Tree* onto the return cart and lowered her voice. "But don't tell her I said so."

That's why Nan insisted on the classics. She said books were like fellow travellers, and if I were going to keep company with someone else's imaginings, she didn't want it to be sentimental claptrap.

"I think you'll discover," Nan said, draping an arm across my shoulders, "that there are some book people you'll love more than regular people."

I blinked hard. "Are there book people you love more than me?"

Nan gave a dry snort. "Celia, you're the living embodiment

of a book person. As if you strolled right off the page and onto my lap."

I leaned into her, blushing at the compliment. Nan knew me too well. We were two book people snuggled under a blanket, whiling away our time. I glanced up to her with adoration. "Do you ever sneak into my room when I'm not there and talk to Captain Ahab?" He was one of my favourite book people. Ever since Nan read Moby Dick to me, Captain Ahab and Queequeg have lived on my sailboat bed.

"No," she said, a smile playing at the edges of her mouth.

Somehow I didn't believe her; Captain Ahab had a way with older women. I snuggled closer and inhaled Nan's essence. Luckily for me she smelled better than Anna Karenina, who was languishing in the root cellar.

Nan was the only person in Happy Valley who understood how I could drift between storybook people and breathing ones, and knew that any time, day or night, they could fill my empty spaces and sit silently with me in my loneliness. Even Archibald, when we were still friends, couldn't do that. If I ever snuck into her house in the middle of the night to shake her awake so she could help me sit in my gloom, she'd likely scream bloody murder. Then punch me in the head.

Nan interrupted my musings. "A penny for your thoughts."

I shrugged. There weren't enough pennies in the world to cover my misery. Even with Nan's extra readings, I didn't know how I was going to manage the rest of second grade. No best friend. No one to play with on my sailboat bed with Captain Ahab. And to top it all off, my teacher, Miss Dobbs, hated me. She never said it out loud, except when she was giving a spelling test. *Hate. I hate Celia Canterberry. H-a-t-e.* And that wasn't the worst of it. Guess who her new pet was? Yep. The Usurper. Eugenia Whitford.

Nan paused and waggled an eyebrow before scanning a

page in *The Scarlet Pimpernel*. "Where did we leave Lady Blakeney?"

I let out a deep breath. "I don't want to hurt your feelings, Nan, but Lady Blakeney is disappointing." I didn't tell her that Captain Ahab agreed. Last night on my sailboat bed, when the moon peeked between the bedsheet sails I'd tied to the curtain rod, Captain Ahab chewed the inside of his cheek. "Some of the books your nan reads you—you know, with fainting women that are all fluff and curls—well, the lot of them could curdle milk." He slipped a knife out of his pocket and began sharpening a willow stick. "Where are the women who took up the sword? Stormed castles? Slipped in and out of the shadows, not leaving a track in their wake?"

I shrugged. "Nan doesn't want to give me any ideas."

Captain Ahab went quiet for a long time. "Queequeg"—that's what he called me— "Queequeg, let me tell you something. If you need ideas, I'm your man."

Nan grunted. "I thought you were enjoying *The Scarlet Pimpernel*?"

"The Pimpernel, yes. But his wife is supposed to be the most witty and clever woman in the world, and I haven't laughed once. And if she's so clever, why does she do such stupid things?"

Nan sucked her teeth. "You may have a point. But you must remember things were different back then. Women didn't have the right to vote, make their own decisions or have their own money. Men ruled the roost. Our world has changed, and so have our women."

"Just like *The Giving Tree*." I was starting to hate that book.

"For the most part." There was hesitation in Nan's voice. "But not all women fit that mold. There was Emmeline Pankhurst, Marie Curie, and Jane Austen. Remember *Pride and Prejudice*?"

I nodded.

"That was Austen at her finest. We'll read more from her. And we shouldn't forget Nahdeste, Geronimo's wise sister. And of course Boudicca."

"Boudicca." The name caught on my earlobe and swung itself into my brain. "Who was she?"

"Queen of the Celts, a fierce warrior. She gave Rome a run for its money."

I said her name again. "I bet Captain Ahab would like her."

"I'm afraid Boudicca might make short work of Captain Ahab." Nan cleared her throat. "Are you ready to hear more of Sir Percy Blakeney and Marguerite St. Just?"

I nodded. Despite my disappointment in Lady Blakeney, my curiosity got the best of me.

"*Marguerite listened—half-dazed as she was—to the fast-retreating, firm footsteps of the four men.*

"*All nature was so still that she, lying with her ear close to the ground, could distinctly trace the sound of their tread, as they ultimately turned into the road, and presently the faint echo of the old cart-wheels, the halting gait of the lean nag, told her that her enemy was a quarter of a league away. How long she lay there she knew not. She had lost count of time; dreamily she looked up at the moonlit sky, and listened to the monotonous roll of the waves.*"

As Nan read, my mind wandered. Boudicca was shuffling through my thoughts, finding a place where Captain Ahab hadn't taken up residence. They would make a formidable pair. This should have made me jump for joy, but it didn't. What if Boudicca looked around, was unimpressed, and decided not to take up residence? What if she caught a whiff of Eugenia and preferred her, just like Archibald did? What if she convinced Captain Ahab to weigh anchor and heave ho off to the Whitfords'? Poor Queequeg would be devastated. But not as much as me.

Celia Should have been

2

As soon as Nan tucked me in and turned out the light, I slipped my hand under my pillow and retrieved my flashlight. On my headboard, right under where I'd carved *Celia Should-Have-Been*, I'd scratched a to-do list. I ran my fingertips over the etchings and felt just as sad inside as I had the night I'd carved it.

1. Get Nan's house back.

Which you'd know, if you've been paying attention, already happened.

2. Find a new best friend.

To replace Archibald who abandoned me for Eugenia Whitford.

3. What's a Luger?

Fanny Figgler, Skinny's mother and my great aunt, used that word, Luger, when she came to blows with Nan. It caused Nan all kinds of grief and piqued my curiosity. But whenever we play the dictionary game, I'm not brave enough to bring it up.

4. What was on my should-have-been's note?

That was the note my should-have-been pa forced me to

give the mayor. He could have given it himself, but he was in the clink at the time.

5. Stop Skinny from marrying Mrs. Willoughby, and sic him on Miss Dobbs.

Mrs. Willoughby is Archibald's mom—Willoughby being her most recent married name—and Miss Dobbs is my afore-mentioned second-grade teacher. Skinny Figgler is a shiftless layabout.

6. Am I an apple?

My should-have-been pa claimed an apple didn't fall far from the tree. If so, I'd rather be an orange.

7. Is she my forever Nan?

That's pretty self-explanatory.

The first thing on my list—get Nan's house back—was crossed off. My should-have-beens had given Nan an ultima-tum: she could keep her house or have legal custody of me. Nan didn't even have to think about it. She chose me; her house went on the auction block. And before my should-have-beens could protest, Old Lady Griggs had purchased it, lock, stock, and barrel, for two buttons. A heavy price when one considered that those buttons used to be the eyes of Griggs' dead husband's effigy. It sounds a bit off, but if you knew Griggs, and lived in Happy Valley, you wouldn't think so.

The next thing on the list—find a new best friend—was what I focused on now. It almost killed me to think it. Archibald was irreplaceable. The best friend a girl could have. To comfort myself, I picked up a dust bunny by his invisible dust-bunny ears and rubbed him on my cheek. What else was I supposed to do? Archibald would never play on my sailboat bed again. Never again would I have the opportunity to scold her when she wept uncontrollably at an impromptu sleepover. It was almost too much to bear.

I felt Captain Ahab's breath on my cheek. "Queequeg," he

said, using my sailboat name. "It pains me to say this, but I think you're up a creek without a paddle."

My head dropped onto my pillow. He was right. I'd been reduced to nothing more than the empty stump of a giving tree. The window pane rattled, and from somewhere outside I swear I could hear the leafless trees sob.

3

Before Nan handed me my lunch pail and sent me off to school, she said the same thing she did every morning. *Don't dawdle.* And *time and school bells don't wait for any man*, or in my case, little girl. I rolled my eyes. I never dawdled. I explored, prodded, and rummaged. Dawdling was for folks that had nothing better to do with their time. Folks that let grass grow under their feet. I would never be one of them.

So on my way to school, when I made a detour to Old Lady Griggs' house, I didn't think I was breaking any of Nan's rules. No one dawdled with Griggs; they were too busy ducking and weaving. Besides, I was avoiding the inevitable—school. Nan never said anything about avoidance.

"Oh, there you are." Griggs peeked between the sheets she was hanging on the line. "I was hoping you'd drop by."

The hair stood up on the back of my neck, because Griggs rarely waited for anyone. "Hoping for what?"

She picked up her empty laundry basket and made her way to her doorstep. "Everyone in town knows that Archibald has tossed you aside for that nasty Eugenia Whitford. I read it myself in the latest edition of *The Canterberry Tales.*"

The Canterberry Tales was a comic strip and the bane of my existence. Griggs had shown it to me the first time Nan allowed her to babysit. Griggs was supposed to be shielding me from a world full of misery, guarding my innocence as if it were the Crown Jewels. But that was too blasé for Griggs. Instead, she had me sit down beside her on her plastic-covered chesterfield, as if we were going to have a cuddle. Then she pulled out a big black scrapbook she'd stashed underneath it, and started flipping the pages. Her lazy eye burrowed into me as my legs welded themselves to the plastic covering. Those pages were full of yellowing newsprint featuring my very own comic strip, *The Canterberry Tales*—a strip Oswald Elliot started writing about me the day I was born. As Mayor Forde had said, if Quintland, a place in Ontario that caged five little girls, could make a boatload of money off the Dionne quintuplets, then why couldn't Happy Valley get its pound of flesh off of one little old abandoned baby? And so, for the past seven years, that's what Oswald Elliot had devoted his life to. That, and courting Miss Dobbs. The two of them used to be curling lot lovers.

That's when Griggs started sharing with me parts of my life from my comic strip existence that Nan cared not to repeat. I flipped through the memories as best I could, naturally filling in the parts that were foggy.

"Your should-have-been ma," Griggs had said, her lazy eye bulging, "is something else. Never left a stone unturned, and not because she was any more successful than Syphilis."

She meant *Sisyphus*, because he's the one that rolled the stone uphill, but I learned long ago it didn't always bode well for me if I interrupted Griggs when she got going. On the bright side though, her pronunciation was getting better.

"But," Griggs had forged on, "that woman never knew where she might find loose change. Your nan hoped she'd shed her wild ways and one day be a teacher or a nurse. Someone respectable. But your should-have-been shed nothing but you. She grew up to be a scrounger. And she's pretty good at it. Scrounged up that man of hers. Don't know what rock she found him under, and if you ask me, she'd be wise to put him back."

We both turned to the comic strip of my hospital birth. That was the first time I saw a drawing of my should-have-been parents. Nan didn't keep a photo of them in the house. Seeing my should-have-been ma, all ragged and howling at the moon, rustled something inside of me. Made me want to scratch her behind the ear like some mangy dog. Griggs said that someone only had to look at my should-have-been ma to know she was a natural-born villain. "She has all the attributes. Her unwashed clothes are in tatters, I'm sure, like other derelict hippies, and she has underarm hair down to her elbows. God only knows the last time she was checked for lice."

In Griggs' mind, those things were damning enough, but what pushed her over the edge was that my should-have-been rejected a perfectly good baby. (Me!) "Granted," she said, "your head was a bit dinted in, and you were conceived on the wrong side of the sheets, but who am I to judge? My parents didn't even have sheets."

I shrugged. Griggs had been judging my should-have-beens for longer than I'd been alive, so why would she question herself now?

She pointed back to the strip. "Your should-have-been ma was the villain, but these high-cheek-boned nurses, on the other hand—they were the heroines. Just look at them, those poor sweet dears. As much as Oswald Elliot gets on my last nerve, he captured the essence of their souls. '*The Virtuous nurses, those unfortunate lambs, try to decide what to do next. They whisper and bleat to one another, for the fate of a young life depends on their next move.*'"

I rolled my eyes. To me it looked like my scrounger should-have-been ma was the only one there with a brain. She must have hated *The Giving Tree* as much as Nan, because she didn't wait for a man to tell her what to do. My should-have-been pa tried, told her to hurry up. Like having a baby was the same as trying on a new dress. But she spat venomous words at him. It was their very own demented Romeo and Juliet scene. The one Shakespeare hadn't been brave enough to write.

With her hair matted to her forehead, our wayward villainess grunts and groans. Between contractions she climbs out of her hospital bed and staggers to the window. 'Keep your pants on, fool. If you'd done that in the first place we wouldn't be here now, would we?'

Her partner in crime, stationed in the parking lot below, takes another swig from his bottle and an extra hard pull on his cigarette. He blows big puffs of blue smoke while the banshee hollers.

Leaving the memory of my inauspicious birth, I turned back to Griggs. "I never saw it," I said, meaning the recent strip about Archibald dumping me. Sweat ran down the length of my back.

"Just because you don't see something doesn't make it any less true." She fished around in her apron pocket until she found what she wanted. "I wouldn't have believed it myself, Archibald changing friends midstream, but here it is in black and white." Griggs laid the cut-out strip on her wooden step.

I sat down beside her and took it in. It was everything she said it would be. Except for one thing—I was pretty. I didn't have my usual seasonal head, a changing cranium for every occasion. At Halloween I had a pumpkin head; at Easter, an egg. I hardly recognized myself. Disappointment filled me. How would anyone know me? Where was my *je ne sais quoi*? My seasonal head was the only thing that set me apart from the riffraff, but I seemed to be the only one concerned about that nugget.

"I think this one is the best one yet. It's almost Shakespeari-an." Griggs cleared her throat and began to read in her Agnes Obermeyer voice. "*Despite her lowly status, Celia Canterberry manages to make one meagre friend. One daring child willing to forgo public scrutiny and face the withering looks of her countrymen. And this friend? Who could she be? None other than the steadfast Archibald Quigley, a scabby-kneed foundling that clings faithfully to Celia's side.*"

The accompanying strip showed Archibald and me sitting cross-legged in dandelion-sprinkled grass, little chickadees landing on our outstretched hands. I couldn't help but smile.

"*But sadly, all good things must come to an end, and so it was with Celia Canterberry and Archibald Quigley.*"

In the next frame, Eugenia Whitford steps between us, her huge head blocking the sun. Archibald shrinks to half her size as Eugenia picks her up by the scruff of her neck, unhinges her jaw, and swallows her whole.

I gasped.

"Upsetting, I know," Griggs said, rubbing my back. "But that's how you win the Pulitzer Surprise, saying so much with so little. The truth will set you free." She paused. "Except Archibald Quigley; for her it only goes from bad to worse."

"Oswald did this?"

"Why do you ask?"

I shrugged. "He's usually more verbose."

"Well, I can't speak to his verboseness." Griggs reddened. "I don't think he's ever talked about it publicly. That's a private matter between him and his doctor. But as for the strip, it looks legitimate to me."

"He didn't sign it. He always signs it."

"Maybe he ran out of ink. Besides, no one else has questioned its legitimacy. Not even Mrs. Jasmine."

"Mrs. Jasmine from the bakery?"

"Yes, from the bakery. What other Mrs. Jasmine do you think I'm talking about?"

I shrugged.

"Well, as I was saying, she was floored when I showed her. Said that you've had enough disappointments in your life, that you didn't need this." Griggs paused for a moment, as if debating whether she should go on. "On the other hand, she said it was good for Archibald to move up in the world. Have to admire the woman. It's very Zen, you know, taking the good with the bad."

I didn't know how to respond to that.

"But I think I can help." Griggs folded the strip and put it back in her apron pocket. "Took this out of the library as soon as I heard. It's Dale Carnegie's *How to Win Friends and Influence People*."

"It sounds boring."

"You hit the nail on the head, sister. It is, dull as dishwater. Not like the books your nan reads you. No torrid love affairs or people running for their lives. To be honest, I don't know how he got the dang thing published. There aren't even any decent pictures. If you search between the boring bits though, he did make a few good points." She placed her gnarled hand on my shoulder. Her lazy eye narrowed. "And I thought I should share some with you."

"Why?"

"Because I care, silly. We, your nan and I—although we haven't talked about it—we need to get you out of this I-don't-have-any-friends-because-I'm-unlikeable rut." Her lazy eye went back to its regular size, and she blinked like Bambi just before his mother got shot.

I blinked back. I wasn't in an unlikeable rut. I was in a looking-for-a-new-best-friend *slump*. But there had to be a new one just around the corner. It was only a matter of finding them. As we spoke, they were probably practicing their Frankenstein-walk, or pining for spring rains so they could sift through mud puddles for waterlogged earthworms. I was pretty sure I could feel my heart straining towards theirs.

Besides, who was Old Lady Griggs to call me unlikeable? Old Lady Griggs, who kept a life-sized effigy of her dead husband at her kitchen table. Said he was better company there; a softer touch than a cold headstone in a windswept graveyard. Still, she expected all who crossed her threshold to give him a nod, same as they had when he was warm and breathing. Old Lady Griggs, who still pranced around town in her honeymoon hat, hoping the plastic flowers made her pruney old skin look as fresh as a daisy. All these things sat on the tip of my tongue, knocking on my teeth to get out. I clamped my jaw tightly.

Griggs rapped me on the head with her knuckles. "If you're not going to pay attention, Celia, I can find far better ways to spend my time."

Rubbing the spot, I snapped. "I *am* paying attention."

The excitement in Griggs' voice was palpable. "Good. It's right here," she said, flipping the book open to a dog-eared page.

"Is that book from the library?" I asked. "I thought you were banned for life for gluing the pages of the dictionary together."

Griggs bristled. "I was. Someone has to think of the children looking up all those dirty words, and it sure as shit isn't going to be the librarian. I snuck in while Miss Libby was on a bathroom break." Griggs tapped her nose like what she was about to divulge was on the down-low. "That woman has borborygmus. I diagnosed her myself. I bet your nan doesn't even know that word. I'm going to use it in the dictionary game one day. Beat your nan fair and square."

"Borborygmus," I said, encouraging Griggs to stay on track.

"Borborygmus," she repeated. "My mother said that's what my father suffered from. His stomach rumbled in the worst way. Made a soul search the sky for rain. Miss Libby's is worse than his though. I followed her into the restroom at church once. But only once. Whatever she did in there made the plastic flowers on my honeymoon hat wilt. I think it's why she's still a Miss." She jabbed the page again.

I looked to where she was pointing. Deep lines of red ink scarred the page. "I don't think you're supposed to underline passages."

"And who made that rule?" Griggs' lazy eye protruded. "You? Your nan?"

"No. I think the library did."

She waved the book dismissively. "Stupid rule. If someone'd had the forethought to highlight the best parts, it wouldn't have taken me a month of Sundays to get through this snooze fest."

Leaning in, I examined the page more closely. I'd seen Griggs' deft hand on my comic strip alterations, the ones she made when Oswald Elliot failed to capture my essence, but I didn't know that with a little red ink and a few stick figures in the margins, she could bring a book as boring as Dale Carnegie's *How to Win Friends & Influence People* to life. I marveled at how that woman could do almost anything with a simple pencil. In fact, her images were so delightful I was almost tempted to show Captain Ahab. Almost. He abhorred stick figures. They reminded him too much of Anna Karenina.

But that's when I thought about the *Dick and Jane* readers in Miss Dobbs' classroom. If any book needed livening up it was that one. How many times could Jane watch Dick jump and not want to beat him to a pulp? See Jane kick Dick. See Dick pull Jane's hair. Griggs would save the day. Miss Dobbs might even let me bring her in for Show and Tell.

"Let's start here." Griggs jabbed a finger at the first underlined sentence. *"Begin in a friendly way."* She paused to let the words sink in. "Doesn't that sound nice? Even you can do that."

I made a face.

"Honestly, Celia, it's easy-peasy. Just like taking a breath of fresh air, or a baby duck in the rain."

"You lost me with the duck."

Her lazy eye wobbled while her ambitious eye bore down on me. "I'll be blunt then. Put it in a way that even you can understand. Don't snort or ball your hands into fists. You're too puny for it to be truly intimidating. And don't get me started on the way you stomp your feet. It's an embarrassment. A stomp should be thunderous, a message from the gods, not a measly little tap. Like your legs are made of glass and might crack if you put a little effort in. Your forebears would roll over in their graves."

"Which ones?"

"The skinny ones." Her brows touched and I knew there was something more she wanted to say, but I wasn't sure I wanted to hear it. I thought of plugging my ears with my fingers but knew she'd only talk louder. "Listen, Celia. This is the last piece of advice I'm going to give you today. For God's sake, don't tell everyone that you can have no better friend than me. It's off-putting. Too much pressure."

Now I really wanted to stomp my feet, or better yet, stick out my tongue. My forebears would probably get a kick out of that, but not Nan. She'd lose her mind. I curled my lip instead. "I've never told anyone that."

"That's where you're wrong. It's been implied. I've seen it in your eyes."

I wanted to protest, but Griggs had moved on to other matters. She was too busy going over her instructions to notice my silent defiance. Telling me how, if I listened to her, I could attract a multitude of friends. "Tomorrow morning," she said, "you can pop by and we can go over how it went. Tweak what didn't work, do more of what did." And with that she shooed me off.

I turned back and looked at her as I headed off to school. She looked triumphant, as if she'd solved all my problems. Little did she know they were just beginning.

4

Griggs' advice didn't make walking to school any less dismal. How was I supposed to "begin in a friendly way"? It was hard to be friendly when most people annoyed me. In frustration, I crunched my way forward, stepping on as many fallen leaves as I could. One crunch for Archibald, two for Eugenia. But I didn't grind the leaves under my heel, which would go against everything Griggs had been trying to teach me.

I crunched all the way to the schoolyard of the Happy Valley School for Reluctant Children. No matter what anyone said, that school did its best to make the children live up to its name. A few more crunches and I joined a long line of fellow stragglers. We snaked our way along the fenceline that separated the Happy Valley Penitentiary from the schoolyard, shuffling our feet and kicking rocks along the way. We didn't speak to one another, hardly looking up from our drudgery. It was like walking the gauntlet. The prison men, fingers threaded through the chain-link fence, hooted and hollered as we passed. For the most part I ignored them. When I'd been in the first grade, things were different. I was tempted to stop and chat, get an inmate to go over the spelling list I neglected to study the night before. But Nan forbade even spelling fraternizations.

She said that just because Mayor Forde was a blithering fool for building a prison next to a school, it didn't mean that I had to be one too. That I was to march right into the school without a sideways glance. I never told Nan, but despite my best intentions, my eyes drifted of their own accord.

Whenever a complaint regarding the shared fenceline reached the mayor's office, Mayor Forde would click his tongue. He was generous to a fault when it came to laying blame. "Am I not the God-appointed mayor?" he'd ask. The complainer would nod. "Did you vote for me?" And no matter what the answer, the mayor would shake his head and give the same response. "You knew what you were getting. I suggest you look in the mirror and place the fault where fault is due. Like the Good Book says, 'Take out the telephone pole from your own eye first, and then you'll be able to see well enough to take out the speck from your brother's eye.'"

That usually shut them up.

Besides, the unfortunate proximity of the prison to the school was part of his election platform: 'Saving money in the most unlikely places.' Potholes became inverted speed bumps. Less speeding; not as many speeding tickets. Not as many speeding tickets; happier voters. Happy voters; more work for local mechanics. He used the same logic regarding the shared fence. Financially prudent. Besides sharing a fenceline, the school saved on janitorial and maintenance services. An inmate on day release could sweep the halls of the Happy Valley School for Reluctant Children and be back in his penitentiary bunk before lights out. "And best of all," Mayor Forde bragged, "no transportation costs."

Spotting me in the melee, one inmate shouted, "Hey, kid. You with the seasonal head. Got any smokes?"

Some days the only things I seemed to be known for were my ever-changing cranium and the ignobility of my birth. I stuck out my tongue before I remembered Griggs' advice. *Begin in a friendly way.* I should have smiled first. That's when I saw him. My should-have-been pa. He was whispering in the man's ear. It was humiliating. The only place I could depend on seeing my should-have-been pa was along the prison fenceline.

Sometimes, when Nan wasn't around, Griggs and I would play *What's he in for this time?* Could it be larceny, disorderly conduct, or my favourite—challenging someone to a duel? On this particular occasion, Griggs said it was quite mundane: driving without a licence.

"I'm talking to you, Seasonal-Head," he called after me, before turning to my pa. The two of them howled.

I quickened my pace. The last time my should-have-been pa called me over to the prison fence he'd handed me a note to give to the mayor. I still don't know what the note said, but I wasn't going to give him the opportunity to give me another one. Going to the mayor's office was too much of an ordeal, and I wasn't going to lose any more sleep wondering about the havoc one little piece of paper might cause. I zeroed in on the entrance door, their hoots of laughter chasing after me. Forcing my eyes forward, I didn't look back once.

5

After I hung my sweater on the hook and stowed my lunchbox, I turned towards Miss Dobbs' classroom. And what to my wondering eyes should appear but Miss Dobbs with one hand on Archibald's shoulder and the other on Eugenia's. The schoolmarm looked as pleased as punch as she drooled over Dr. Whitford, Eugenia's father.

"I thought I'd drop them off personally," Dr. Whitford said, leaning in a little too close to the school teacher. "The girls had a sleepover last night. Just thought you should know they are a little tired. Too much fun and giggling. You know how little girls are."

The two scamps, in their matching dresses and hair tied up in yellow-ribboned pigtails, giggled as if on cue.

"Oh, I certainly understand little girls," Miss Dobbs said, almost passing out with delight.

I rolled my eyes. If Oswald Elliot, Happy Valley's esteemed cartoon journalist and Miss Dobbs' former curling parking lot lover, could see her now, he'd give up on his unrealized journalistic dreams and drag her away by her hair.

"I know it's unadvisable," Dr. Whitford went on, "for them

to have a sleepover on a school night, but once I explained to Archibald's mother what a rough time Eugenia was having, and the only thing that brought her comfort was young Archibald, she relented. A mother's loving heart always rules the day."

"Oh, you don't have to be a mother to have a loving heart," Miss Dobbs said, as she cow-kicked me through the classroom door.

Archibald and Eugenia skipped in after me, still giggling, and dripping with gumdrop sweat. It was enough to make me sick. And when Archibald took her seat at the desk in front of mine, she didn't even acknowledge me. I leaned forward and loud-whispered into her ear. "Archibald," I said, remembering to *begin in a friendly way*, "do you want to play hopscotch at recess? I'll let you go first."

She acted like she hadn't heard a word I said.

"Arch-i-bald," I said, with an extra measure of sweetness.

Nothing.

I narrowed my eyes. Griggs didn't know what she was talking about. "One sleepover and you don't even know me," I said. "I bet it wasn't even fun. Did you tromp through Farmer Hempel's pasture at midnight? Get drenched by the worst rainstorm in a century? Have to sing 'Jesus Loves Me' just so you didn't get eaten by witches?"

Silence.

"That's what I thought. Our sleepover was better!"

Archibald shrugged one shoulder, as if she were sloshing off my words. I stared at the back of her head. There was more than one way to skin a cat. Leaning forward, I grabbed one of her crisp yellow hair ribbons and gave it a tug. Nothing. I tugged a little harder. Still nothing. That's when I got the bright idea of tying a pencil to that dangling yellow abomination. More a matter of convenience than anything else. That way I'd never have to rummage through my desk for a writing implement.

But Archibald couldn't even do that for me. She ripped out the pencil and rocketed it over her shoulder. My heart almost stopped. She could have taken out my eye.

"Those things don't grow on trees," I hissed, before putting up my hand. "Miss Dobbs, did you see that?"

"What?" Miss Dobbs asked, as if she'd been blind to the whole thing.

"Archibald threw a pencil at me."

"Well, if she did, I'm sure she had her reasons." Miss Dobbs clip-clopped to Archibald's desk and gave her one of the muffins she usually reserved for Eugenia. So much for beginning in a friendly way.

When Miss Dobbs was back in front of the classroom, she spread her arms wide, like Maria in *The Sound of Music*. "Good morning class," she cooed. "Isn't it a wonderful day to be alive?"

No one said anything, fearing a trick question, but our dreamy-eyed teacher didn't seem to notice. She went on and on about the crisp fall air and the cool autumn sun. I'm sure most of us thought her cheeriness was due to an aneurysm, or early-morning shots in the staffroom. But that's when she did the most unexpected thing.

She twirled.

The wide-eyed class froze. This was not the Miss Dobbs we were used to. The Miss Dobbs we were used to never said good morning. She never threw her arms open wide unless she was swinging a yardstick. And as for the twirling, it was unnatural. Akin to no snow at Christmas, or Old Lady Griggs being the belle of the ball. The twirling was so unexpected that Timmy Crybaby-Head emptied his entire bladder and nearly slid out of his seat.

But her joy didn't stop there, Miss Dobbs twirled as she mopped. She spun so much that little droplets of watery urine speckled the children unlucky enough to be in Crybaby-Head's immediate vicinity. And to top it all off, Miss Dobbs didn't even get cross at Timmy for making the mess. It made me want to get out of my desk and shake her. Take the mop away and tell her she was traumatizing children in a whole new way. One sniff from their parents and she'd have a stampede of complaints. But my contempt for the woman prevented me from getting involved. In fact, at recess I was going to encourage Timmy Crybaby-Head to take an extra-long drink from the water fountain.

"I need to paint my nails," Miss Dobbs blurted, as if it were a national emergency. She went a little white in her cheeks as she waved her hand before the class so we could all see the chipped nail on her right index finger. "Can't be caught unprepared again. You never know when some newly widowed father might saunter down the hall and peek in. See me teaching my beloved students, every inch of my flawlessness impeccable." She winked at Eugenia, as if it were a coded message only she could understand. "And while my nails dry we'll have USSR. Won't that be fun?"

Uninterrupted Sustained Silent Reading. There was a communal groan, and Miss Dobbs did another twirl while handing out the *Dick and Jane* readers, just like some stupid Disney princess.

"Hey, Bluebird Girl," I said, beginning in a friendly way. "As much as we all love USSR, I don't think anybody wants to read today. Can't concentrate with all our concern over your chipped nail." The class nodded around me. "Can we play with plasticine instead?"

Miss Dobbs scrunched her nose and didn't even seem to notice that I'd called her Bluebird Girl. "I suppose this one time...," she sing-songed.

Playing with plasticine at an undesignated time was unheard of. Miss Dobbs was a stickler when it came to keeping to the timetable, marking out the day to the exact minute. The shock of the schedule change momentarily paralyzed the class, but once they got over the astonishment of it, there was a flurry of movement. Kids crawled over one another to be first to the plasticine shelf. I stood back and watched—it was a thing of wonder. Arms and legs flailing, children squealing and grunting. This was the way Grade Two was meant to be. Inhaling a deep breath, I threw caution to the wind and waded into the free-for-all.

Taking a big ball of red plasticine, I began kneading it, making it pliable with my deft hands. What to make? What to make? That's when I came up with the bright idea to make two telephones—one for me and one for Archibald. If she refused to talk to me in person, I'd have to give her a call. I fashioned the two phones with a long snake wire to connect them, just like the kind Mike and Nancy Karr had on *The Edge of Night*. When they were almost exact replicas, I leaned forward and placed one on Archibald's desk. She ignored it. I put my red receiver to my ear and I brrringed it.

"Brrring, brrring," I trilled. "Brrring."

Archibald crossed her arms as if she hadn't heard my brrringing. I brrringed again. At my final attempt, Eugenia Whitford rose from her seat, raised a fist high in the air, and squashed my plasticine telephone.

"It's out of service," she squawked, with a malicious smile plastered on her freckled face.

I didn't say anything. Instead I thinned my lips, rolled my red plasticine telephone into a ball, and beaned Eugenia Whitford in the forehead. The ball didn't even bounce just dropped to the floor like a lead balloon. At first Eugenia stood there agog probably trying to figure out a response befitting Happy Valley's beloved doctor's daughter. She settled on hysteria. She bellowed so loudly it was impossible to hear the mice fleeing across the cork ceiling tiles. The whole thing sounded a lot like bedlam.

Miss Dobbs lurched in her twisty teacher chair, spilling red nail polish all over her crisp white blouse. Her eyes blackened, and I knew the witch-demon was back—the one who'd eaten that poor little bluebird girl in one gulp. "What happened?" Miss Dobbs thundered, while waving her freshly painted fingernails in the air.

Dry-eyed Eugenia, in mid-bellow, pointed in my direction.

No words accompanied the accusation. For my part, I leaned over and pretended to tie my shoe. Miss Dobbs wasn't fooled. I'd used that ruse before. She bore down on me with all the fervour of a gold-digging schoolmarm. "Celia Canterberry, what have you done?"

I looked from Miss Dobbs to Eugenia. There was no easy way out, I had to tell the truth. "I thought she wanted my plasticine ball," I said. "It's not my fault she can't catch. Isn't that right, Archibald?"

Archibald put her hands over her ears and started rocking back and forth—which wasn't very useful when Miss Dobbs grabbed hold of my ear and frog-marched me to the front of the classroom. "This day started so well," she said. "There was promise in the air. But you," she gave my ear a shake, "couldn't leave well enough alone. You had to let your green-eyed jealousy rear its ugly head. Can't acknowledge that Archibald has made a better friend and left you in the dust."

Eugenia's wails lessened as Miss Dobbs scolded me, so she wouldn't miss a word of the reprimand. Her owl eyes blinked in blameless wonder, as if never in her wildest dreams had she imagined Miss Dobbs had a dark side. She seemed to forget all about her welty forehead. Her sole focus was on me, and how Miss Dobbs was chewing me up and spitting me out.

"You are just like your mother!"

I gasped.

"Tell her why she's like her mother." Eugenia had inched up on us, until her voice slithered into Miss Dobbs' ear.

Miss Dobbs blinked, and I knew she had been thrust back into the trauma of grade school, stranded high on the teeter-totter by Audrey, my should-have-been ma, whose feet were planted firmly on the ground. I could almost hear the taunts. *What ya going to do about it, smarty pants? Go tell the teacher? She doesn't care. Nobody does.* Old Lady Griggs had told me that, as a child, my mother had bullied Miss Dobbs for years. Whenever Miss Dobbs looked at me, no matter what I said, I wondered if all she heard were the old taunts of my should-have-been ma.

Miss Dobbs broadened her chest. "This time," she said, "somebody *does* care, and there isn't a thing you can do about it, Audrey Canterberry!" Clearly, Miss Dobbs heard the taunts in my head too.

She gave my ear another tug, and I blinked back tears. No one called me Audrey. Not even when Nan was ready to skin me alive did she confuse me with that wretch. In fact, when my should-have-been pa said that the apple didn't fall too far from the tree, Nan had blown a gasket. She said that my should-have-beens were not trees, nor was I an apple. But from the look on Miss Dobbs' face, she wasn't seeing me as an apple or a tree. The only thing she saw me as was Audrey, her bully and tormentor.

Just loud enough for the class to hear, but not so loud that it broke Miss Dobbs out of her spell, Eugenia began to sing. "Last night I heard my mama singing a song."

And from her desk, Archibald quietly responded with the "ooh wees" and chirpy chorus.

"Woke up this morning and my mama was gone," Eugenia returned.

Archibald put in her two bits again.

Now I knew what they'd been doing at their sleepover. They were practicing the worst song on the radio. The one Nan hated. Whenever it aired, she'd turn down the volume and say that even though she enjoyed most forms of music, she couldn't sanction nonsense. I knew it was not about sanctioning nonsense; it was about my should-have-beens. She didn't want me to be reminded of my abandonment with some catchy little ditty.

I wanted to kick both those girls in the shins, even though when it came to the last bit, *Where's your papa gone? Far far away*, Archibald was sobbing so hard she was blowing snot bubbles. My heart melted. I knew she still cared. If we'd still been friends, I'd have let her wipe her nose on my shirt.

The kids around me began to twitch. Even for Eugenia Whitford, this was a bridge too far. I crossed my arms and waited. Miss Dobbs had to intervene and put her little minion on notice. But that's not what happened. First Miss Dobbs' head began to bob and her shoulders swayed. I knew it was only a matter of time before she asked the class to join in on the chorus. It made me want to punch them both in the stomach. At least that wouldn't leave a mark.

Miss Dobbs gave one last sway before she shook off her stupor. "We need to be kind to each other," she said. "I told Dr. Whitford that I had a loving heart, probably even more so than Lacey Willoughby, Archibald's mother. And unlike her, I don't have any stretch marks. He needs to know that I could take care of his sweet Eugenia, same as his dead wife." Her bottom lip quivered. "And now look at her." She let go of my ear and cupped Eugenia's chin in her palm. "One morning with Celia, and her lovely face is ruined."

As if on cue, Eugenia forgot her *Where's your mama gone* song and resumed her wailing. The redness in her face deepened but never quite caught up to the forehead welt that looked like an all-seeing eye.

"How am I going to explain this to her father?" Miss Dobbs went on. "He entrusted me with his most prized possession. And instead of protecting it, I painted my nails."

I wanted to tell Miss Dobbs that I was Nan's most prized possession, and look where that got me. But I knew it would be a waste of breath. Miss Dobbs seemed hypnotized by Eugenia's red welt, acting like the fate of the world depended on what she would do next. As soon as she came to her senses, she sent Archibald to the water fountain and told her to wet a fistful of paper towels.

"We need to get the swelling down," Miss Dobbs said, placing the glob of wetness on the raised mark. Eugenia shuddered as her doe eyes gazed gratefully into Miss Dobbs'. "I know what we'll do," Miss Dobbs' said, her voice rising over Eugenia's whimpers. "Remember last week when I told you we were going to do presentations at the Halloween Spooktacular? We'll divide into groups now. And each group will be responsible for a short presentation on a person in our neighbourhood. And not just any kind of person. We want the people who inspire. The people who actually get dressed in the morning, leave the house, and make a difference. Professionals. Keep in mind that if what they do doesn't make anyone envious, they're probably not worth talking about." Miss Dobbs raised her eyebrows and looked around the room long enough for her words to sink in. Then she patted Eugenia on the cheek. "And you, my dear, can choose the groups."

Eugenia's whimpering abruptly ended, as if at those words health flowed back into her. She surveyed her kingdom, clapping her hands and squealing.

"I knew you'd be pleased," Miss Dobbs said.

With her hands folded behind her back, Eugenia began

pacing up and down the rows, her all-seeing eye reminding us that we would forever be under her gaze. "Archibald will obviously be my partner. With our matching dresses we're practically sisters."

Archibald blew one last snot bubble before laying her head on her desk.

Miss Dobbs wrote the combination down in her book.

"And Sally Shephard will be," Eugenia put a finger to her chin thoughtfully, "partners with Billy Billboson." She paced up and down the rows calling names while Miss Dobbs, following closely, wrote down every word the little succubus uttered. "And Lenard will be Bartholomew's." After she'd covered the room, she stood before me. "That leaves Celia Canterberry. Let me see, let me see." Eugenia scanned the classroom. Her face looked disappointed, as if leaving me without a partner pained her. Then she brightened, like something marvellous had just occurred to her. "Celia Canterberry's partner will be Timmy Leach."

"That's perfect," Miss Dobbs shrilled, as if Eugenia couldn't have done a better job.

I looked at Timmy Leach, otherwise known as Timmy Crybaby-Head, and fell into the depths of despair. He would have been my last choice. I'd rather have been partnered with Sally Shephard and her burgeoning moustache. Her only vice was the tin of Captain Fawcett's moustache wax in her desk. Or Billy Billboson and his three strands of hair: Larry, Moe and Curly. He didn't have any vices; he was too busy patting down his ineffectual comb-over. At least then I could have been clumped in with the regular kids. The ones no one really noticed, who could walk in and out of a room with faces that were rarely remembered. With Timmy, who played with dead flies and left a dribbling yellow trail, my humiliation as a true outsider was complete.

"And since you're partners now, Celia," Miss Dobbs said, with sunbeams in her voice, "you can be responsible for Timmy's dribbling. The mop is in the supply closet."

I looked from Crybaby-Head to the closet, and wondered how many times I'd have to make the trip. My feet were already sore. I should have thrown that plasticine ball harder.

Sense
and
Sensibility
Jane Austen

6

"Nan is starting *Sense and Sensibility* tonight," I told Griggs when she popped over after supper.

"Bully for you," Griggs said. Her eyes darted from Nan to me. "It must be nice."

"It is." I nudged the chrome chair closer to the table. "Nan doesn't do voices like you do when you read my comic strip, which is a little bit disappointing, but her overall dramatic interpretation is admirable."

Griggs bit her lip before she turned her face to the wall. I waited for her to come back into herself. "I remember when your nan read me *Beautiful Joe*," she said, her voice quivering like Agnes Obermeyer's when she was being pummelled in the street by her sister. "Do you remember that, Molly?"

Nan nodded.

"I loved that book." Her voice broke into the whimsical tone of the town baker, Mrs. Jasmine. "It broke my heart, the way they called Joe a cur, and his first master beat and mutilated him. I still lose sleep over that dog."

"Nan's never read me that book."

"And I never will. Dorigen was traumatized. Put up posters

all over town. *Have you seen this dog?* She even had the minister announce it from the pulpit."

"You're the one that said it was inspired by a true story." Griggs' words were clipped, and I could have sworn they came straight out of the mouth of Mrs. Whitford. Griggs was outdoing herself. "Don't blame me for taking your word for it."

Nan didn't respond, but I knew she was fuming.

"After that," Griggs said in her regular voice, "your nan never read me another book. Said I was too unpredictable and she didn't want to be responsible for any misunderstandings. Logically, I assumed she only read aloud rarely, like at a funeral, or the occasional road sign, but now it seems it's a regular occurrence. As if *you're* any more reliable."

"I don't make posters," I said.

"No, you just stow sweet Anna Karenina down your dingy cellar and tuck Captain Ahab, a full-grown man, in your sail-boat bed." She raised an eyebrow. "No one finds that strange besides me? The only thing I did was hang up a few well-drawn posters."

Nan and me blinked blankly at Griggs. She had a point. I had my storybook friends, but at least mine stayed put. Anna Karenina lived in the cellar during inclement weather and came out for seeding and harvest, obviously. Captain Ahab was more of a sentimental sort and stuck around for starry nights and windblown days. Griggs' little cur dog wouldn't even lift himself off the page to pretend-lick her face. It was the saddest thing I ever heard, but neither of us were going to dredge it up. Instead, Nan changed the subject. "Have you aged a new casserole?"

Griggs' eyes sparkled. In Happy Valley, she was best known for her shepherd's pie casserole. She'd been lugging that pie around for years, freezing and unfreezing the thing at regular intervals. Church potlucks, birthday parties, and unexpected deaths all were victims of her culinary ineptitude. Anyone with an ounce of sense would thank her profusely, say they had an aversion to shepherd food—or some such nonsense—and enthusiastically give the offering back. Griggs would pop it back into the deep-freeze and wait for the next unwitting sucker. The last time she produced her pie, Fanny Figgler, my not-so-great great-aunt, accidently dashed it upon the ground when she tried to impale Griggs with her broom-handle javelin. And although I knew she wanted to, Griggs didn't stoop so low as to scoop up the pie, blow off the dust, and act like nothing had happened. Hence, the need for her to age a new one.

"It's almost there," Griggs said. "The other day I tried to feed it to Walter's cat. Tiberius took one sniff and lost his cookies."

"You should be proud," Nan said, with a flat voice, "considering what that cat eats."

"You don't have to tell me twice. But what I really want to talk to you about is my television. It's on the fritz. I was hoping you'd climb up on the roof and adjust the antenna."

Nan bristled.

Griggs held up a hand. "And before you object, Molly, just hear me out. We both know my husband's not going to do anything about it. God knows I've tried. He just sits at the kitchen table, his head lolling this way and that, like he doesn't have a care in the world. Only the other day I dragged him out of the house and started boosting him up the ladder, but he went all limp. Made me look like a fool." She looked to Nan and me for some kind of response, but we just blinky-eye stared at her. "And don't get me started on coat hanger rabbit ears," she went on. "They're as useless as tits on a turkey. I get more snow than picture. And the thought of me going on the roof and fixing it myself is out of the question. I could get hurt."

Nan rolled her eyes. She couldn't argue with a word Griggs

said. It was common knowledge that when Mr. Griggs had been a breathing human being—instead of a stuffed and fluffed one —he hadn't been particularly adventurous, or for that matter ambitious. Nan once told me of how, when Mr. Griggs was a younger man, he wouldn't even shovel out his car when it got snowed in. He just called in sick to work. Climbing on his roof to fix an antenna would have been out of the question. It was more likely that he'd amble off to the neighbours and watch their TV.

"And since you're being so obstinate, Molly, and I know the two of you are starting a new book, why don't I stay here and join you? It won't be the Ed Sullivan show, but beggars can't be choosers."

Nan glared at me as if I'd blurted out some state secret. I shrugged. Griggs was oblivious and went on. "We can have popcorn and maybe play a round of the dictionary game."

That was her trump card. If Nan didn't brighten at the prospect of the dictionary game, she wouldn't brighten at anything. The three of us had been playing it as long as I could remember. Nan played it with Griggs on days she wanted to have an easy win. With me, it was for educational purposes. Nan said my naysayers would think twice before tangling with a child who had a larger vocabulary than they did.

"First things first," Nan said. "I don't want any grumbling over who has the best spot. Or criticism of the way I read."

Griggs nodded. "As long as Celia can pee for me, I'm good."

I rolled my eyes. I wasn't going to fall for that old chestnut. "How many times do we have to go over this? One person can't pee for another person." I didn't tell them that I knew it for a fact. That I'd questioned Miss Dobbs about it in science class. She laughed at me for a week. I even heard her tell the other teachers about it when I walked past the staffroom.

But it didn't end there. One day when the school secretary

was sick, Agnes Obermeyer was called in as a substitute. Having no children of her own, Agnes was in her glory with all the zippers to zip and noses to wipe. I'd never seen her look so pleased. But what tickled her most was the school intercom system. Right before first recess, her crackly voice announced, "Celia Canterberry, to the office, please. Principal Wolfe needs to go pee. Celia Canterberry, to the office, please." Up and down the hallway, the teachers roared with laughter. But to Agnes' dismay, she was never asked to sub again. The person who seemed most pleased though, was Timmy Crybaby-Head. He said it explained his dribbling, considering all the pregnant women in the world and the lack of sufficient bathroom facilities.

Griggs shrugged a shoulder. "It was fun while it lasted."

Ignoring Griggs, I pulled up a chair to the stove. "How much popcorn shall we make?"

"Copious amounts," Nan said, after she'd poured the kernels into the aluminum popcorn pot.

Griggs and me grinned at each other. Nan had given the opening salvo. We were playing the dictionary game. Nan would start with a word, and then Griggs and me, in turn, would use a similar word in a sentence. At the thought of all those synonyms, a shiver ran down my spine.

"A bumper crop," Griggs said.

It was my turn. "But not as abundant as last time."

That's when it all went haywire. Griggs' face reddened. "What do you mean *last time*? You made popcorn when I wasn't here?"

I shrugged.

Griggs turned on Nan. "We've been popping corn together for as long as I can remember. We used to call one another the popcorn sisters. Or have you forgotten?"

Nan shook her head.

"And now I find out you've been popping behind my back?"

"I've not been popping behind your back, Dorigen. We're playing a game, remember? Celia was just trying to improve her vocabulary."

Griggs snorted. "Well, at least I didn't lose. None of us made it past round one."

"Oh, God," Nan said, almost under her breath. "Let's get this over with."

Griggs and me trudged into the living room. Nan brought up the rear with all the stuff she had to carry, including the popcorn bowl, glasses of water, and of course the book. While she was gathering her supplies, Griggs whispered, "How did it go? Did you begin in a friendly way?"

I nodded. "But Eugenia got hurt anyway."

"I should have seen that one coming." Griggs pursed her lips, deep in thought. But before she could give further instructions, Nan lumbered in.

"What did I miss?" Nan's voice was laced with suspicion.

Griggs and me looked blankly at one another.

"That's what I thought," Nan said, narrowing her eyes. "You two are up to something."

"Celia wants to have a farting contest," Griggs lied. "She seems to think that, as a book club, it would make us stand out."

I nodded. "But unlike Roland le Peteur, Griggs can't fart on key, so it's kind of a bust."

Nan didn't say anything for a long time. She handed me the popcorn bowl after I had set the glasses of water on the coffee table. Taking the spot between us, her fingers tapped the cover of *Sense and Sensibility*. Her mouth opened and closed again.

Griggs filled in the gap. "First our pot and pan band, and now this..."

I reached over and patted Griggs on the leg. "I guess it wasn't meant to be."

Giving up on having a sensible conversation, Nan cleared her throat and opened *Sense and Sensibility* by Jane Austen.

"The family of Dashwood had long been settled in Sussex. Their estate was large, and their residence was at Norland Park, in the centre of their property, where, for many generations, they had lived in so respectable a manner as to engage the general good opinion of their surrounding acquaintance."

I tried to think of ways to irritate Griggs and kill two birds with one stone, but nothing came to mind until Nan read, *"The constant attention of Mr. and Mrs. Henry Dashwood to his wishes, which proceeded not merely from interest, but from goodness of heart, gave him every degree of solid comfort which his age could receive; and the cheerfulness of the children added a relish to his existence."*

I leaned forward, looked around Nan to Griggs, and mouthed, "That's how Nan feels about me. I add relish to her existence."

Griggs' lazy eye quivered.

Nan kept reading. *"By a former marriage, Mr. Henry Dashwood had one son: by his present lady, three daughters. The son, a steady respectable young man, was amply provided for by the fortune of his mother, which had been large, and half of which devolved on him on his coming of age.*

It was Griggs' turn to lean forward. "Your nan was relishing me long before you ever came along."

"Was not."

"Was so."

Nan slammed the book shut. "What are you two up to?"

Griggs jabbed a sharp finger in my direction. "She started it."

"Started what?"

"How am I supposed to know?" spat Griggs. "Celia's the one smirking."

Nan turned to me and raised an eyebrow.

Not wanting to sound foolish, I stretched the truth. "We were arguing about condiments. Relish to be precise."

"If I'd known we were arguing about condiments," Griggs' hands balled into fists, "I'd have said ketchup."

"This is exactly why I didn't think reading to the two of you was a good idea."

Griggs and me gasped simultaneously. Our intention was only to irritate one another through one-upmanship, not turn Nan off the whole shebang. One-upmanship was something storybook characters did on a regular basis, which, I might add, had never bothered Nan in the past. In fact, she seemed to enjoy their witty banter. But apparently the real-life application was unacceptable. The word *hypocrite* was on the tip of my tongue, but I thought better of it. I wanted to keep the tip of my tongue, thank you very much. Instead, I batted my eyes and tried to look contrite.

Nan's lips thinned, and although I knew it was against her better judgement, she continued. I'm pretty sure she skipped a few paragraphs, though.

"*The whole was tied up for the benefit of this child, who, in occasional visits with his father and mother at Norland, had so far gained on the affections of his uncle, by such attractions as are by no means unusual in children of two or three years old; an imperfect articulation, an earnest desire of having his own way, many cunning tricks, and a great deal of noise, as to outweigh all the value of all the attention which, for years, he had received from his niece and her daughters.*"

Griggs leaned forward and mouthed again. "Cunning tricks. Sounds like you."

I gasped. "Does not."

"Does so."

Nan slapped the book shut. "Do you want me to read? Or are the two of you going to spend the entire evening infuriating me?"

I looked at Griggs. We were both at a loss. Being read to was one of my favourite pastimes. But then again, Nan had never said a whole evening could be devoted to infuriating her before.

"We didn't know we had a choice," Griggs said.

I nodded emphatically.

Nan turned from Griggs to me. "A choice in what?"

"Between being read to and infuriating you."

Nan slammed the book down on the end table before disappearing into the kitchen. "I need an aspirin."

7

Eugenia Whitford was holding court when I slipped into my desk. "This is my Chatty Cathy doll," she said, with the most insipid grin. "My mom bought it for me before she died."

The whole class did an "Awwww," while Eugenia wiped away an invisible tear, and Miss Dobbs placed a comforting hand on her shoulder. I wanted to roll my eyes, but I couldn't bring myself to do it. Since Griggs' *begin in a friendly way* advice didn't work, she told me to try *being genuinely interested in other people.* With my elbows on my desk and my chin cupped in my palms, I faked interest. Besides, I reminded myself, Eugenia's mother did die, whereas the only thing my living, breathing one did was abandon me and steal my birthday money. The thought burned my bum. Even her dead mom was better than mine.

"She can say eleven different phrases," Eugenia prattled on. "Like *I love you, Please take care of me,* or *Let's play school.*"

The class was spellbound. No one had seen a Chatty Cathy before. She was the kind of doll that was circled in a catalogue and begged for at Christmas, but most parents thought she was too ridiculous or expensive to order. Apparently, the late Mrs. Whitford didn't mind ridiculous.

"They don't make them anymore." Eugenia's smugness filled the room. "That's why I keep mine pristine. Daddy says it will be worth a lot of money one day." Her empty eyes scanned the classroom. "Does anybody want to pull her string?"

Hands rocketed into the air. I let out a grunt. Bunch of lick-spittles.

"Let me see, let me see." Eugenia tapped a finger on her chin as she rose on her toes. "Archibald, you can pull Chatty Cathy's string."

Archibald popped out of her desk and was in front of the classroom like a flash, as if she was afraid Eugenia might change her mind and pick some less deserving child. As Archibald pulled, Eugenia gave instructions. "Not too fast. You don't want to rip it out of her body. Pull it gentle, like a good mother would."

Since children didn't come with strings, I wasn't sure which good mother she was talking about.

"I love you," Chatty Cathy said, and Eugenia beamed like the doll meant it.

I raised my hand. "Doesn't every single Chatty Cathy say that? Even if you drop her down an outhouse hole or light her hair on fire?"

Eugenia ignored my question. "She comes with her hair tied up in pigtails, which you can take out and comb anytime you want. And she has this cute little dress, and patent leather shoes with knee socks."

"We can use her as a science experiment," I suggested helpfully. "Because we're here to learn, right? Try chucking her to the floor. See what she has to say then."

Eugenia's eyes flashed. The rest of the class seemed excited about my suggestion, especially the boys. Billy Billboson and

Bartholomew Dankworth argued about who would be the best chucker, while Sally Shephard volunteered to scotch tape any cracks Chatty Cathy's cranium might suffer. I smiled at how marvellously things were turning out. A new respect was building for Griggs' advice from her pilfered library book.

"Enough!" Miss Dobbs' shrill retort vibrated down our spines. "There will be no need to tape anything, as there will be no chucking dolls to the floor."

We trembled in our seats. And that's when I knew. That woman, who dared to call herself a teacher, was trying to suffocate science. She'd be the first to poison Socrates. If she had a string, I'm sure she'd say, *Come have a drink. You look thirsty.*

Miss Dobbs paced the rows of desks, smacking the yardstick in the palm of her hand. When the class was sufficiently petrified, she nodded for Eugenia to continue.

"My father hired a seamstress to make Chatty Cathy and me matching wardrobes." Eugenia's lips pursed with superiority.

It was enough to make me want to puke. If I brought one of these ridiculous dummies home, all my storybook friends would run for the hills. And I'd be stuck with a stupid doll who kept repeating the same eleven things over and over again. Why would anyone in their right mind want a Chatty Cathy doll?

Obviously though, Archibald wasn't in her right mind. As Eugenia spoke, Archibald stroked Chatty Cathy's hair with longing in her eyes. I knew she wanted to grab that baby doll and swaddle her close to her heart. All these years, and I hadn't known the girl. Even Griggs would be mortified to have an exbest friend with such limited ambitions. I put up my hand again. "When is it going to be my turn to talk in front of the class?"

Miss Dobbs blanched. "Your turn? Pray tell, what could you possibly talk about? That is, if you don't include earthworms or witches."

She had me there. My pause was a beat too long, and Miss Dobbs bore down on me. "Do you have a Chatty Cathy doll? Is your father a newly widowed doctor looking for a bride? No?" Her eyebrows arched. "Perhaps you will share with the class where your not-so-esteemed patriarch is currently residing?"

My mouth went dry, but Miss Dobbs' mouth didn't. "In case no one's heard, Celia's father is bunking at the Happy Valley Penitentiary. I'm sure you've all seen him loitering along the fenceline. If you haven't, just imagine Celia in stripes."

My humiliation was complete.

When the class was filing out for recess, I swear Archibald reached a hand towards me before Eugenia smacked it away. "Remember what I told you," Eugenia snapped.

Archibald blinked about a million times. I think it was Morse code for sorry. But I'd have to ask Griggs to pilfer another book from the library to make sure.

Following afternoon recess, Miss Dobbs divided the class into the groups Eugenia had dictated. "Halloween is going to be upon us before we know it," she said. "So we better get cracking."

As I pulled my desk towards Timmy Crybaby-Head's, he pulled his in the opposite direction. It was fine by me. I'd chase him around the classroom all day. It was better than working on some stupid Halloween project called *Who are the people in your neighbourhood?* We should have been drawing ghosts, carving pumpkins, or bobbing for apples—normal Halloweeny stuff. But no. Not us. Miss Dobbs seemed to be of the mind that children would rather stand in front of a crowd and talk about the mailman or the baker. People the audience had seen every day, yet were supposed to marvel at. As if a seven-year-old could scrounge up a useful and brand-new nugget of information. I mean, I could, but not the rest of these numbskulls.

Miss Dobbs slapped her yardstick on my desk. "You're supposed to be working, not playing desk tag with Timmy."

"We're not playing," I snapped back.

"Don't contradict me!"

"I wasn't," I said. "I was *correcting* you."

Apparently, Miss Dobbs was averse to correction. "Celia," she boomed. "Gum. Corner."

"I wasn't chewing gum."

"That's neither here nor there. Peel off a piece from the bottom of your desk and get cracking."

8

I marched straight to Griggs' house after school. "Being genuinely interested in other people didn't work either," I told her, slamming the outside door for punctuation before stepping into her kitchen. She was serving Mr. Griggs his favourite after school snack: orange Freshie and stale cookies. I eyed a cookie. Griggs noticed my hesitation.

"If your teeth are good, it shouldn't be a problem."

I looked from Griggs to her husband. He was no help, sitting there in his overalls and plaid shirt, head lolling to one side. He hadn't taken a bite of one of Griggs' cookies in years, and he was all the more content for it. Still, I had to partake. Either that, or admit I had faulty genes. My should-have-beens were already doing everything in their power to prove that deficiency, and I was the only thing standing in their way. Like the little Dutch boy. I bit down hard. Cookie crumbs sprayed across Griggs' plastic table cloth.

She smiled. "I told your nan they weren't too old and there was no need to throw them out."

I felt used.

"How did it go?" Griggs said, dipping her cookie in her Freshie cup. "With my advice, I mean."

"I already told you. It didn't work. Apparently, people don't care if you're genuinely interested in them."

"I thought as much," she said. "Children are a wily bunch. They don't follow the same rules of decorum as the more civilized older generation." Reaching across the table, Griggs laid her hand on mine. "But let's not throw the baby out with the bathwater. Mr. Carnegie might have something useful to say. After all, he published a book, didn't he?" Reaching into her apron pocket, Griggs pulled out the dog-eared guide. "Let's see, let's see. Dramatize your ideas." Griggs looked up at me. "We can cross that one off our list. Dramatizing got you in the mess you're in." She flipped a few more pages. "How about this one? It says here you should be a good listener; get other people to talk about themselves."

"I can do that."

Griggs looked me up and down. "That remains to be seen."

After Griggs finished giving me my daily dose of Dale Carnegie, I told her I needed her to do me a favour.

"What kind of favour?" Griggs went so still I was afraid she'd stopped breathing.

"Does it matter?"

"It could."

I chose my words carefully. "Can you swipe another book from the library?"

Griggs' face lit up. "With pleasure."

I was still swinging my legs at Griggs' kitchen table when Nan barged in. "There you are," she said, a little out of breath. "I've been looking high and low for you." She seemed cross, and I couldn't figure out what I had done to annoy her this time. It could have been almost anything. That's when she pulled the Happy Valley Journal from her handbag and all was revealed. She pushed aside the Freshie cups and brushed away the cookie crumbs before laying the paper on the table top. Griggs and I examined the latest strip.

"It's a vignette," Griggs said. "Brings the Happy Valley Journal on par with periodicals from Paris and New York." She waved her hand through the air. "I know it's not much, but it's a start."

Nan could have been knocked over by a feather. "A vignette?"

"Yes, a vignette. Honestly, Molly Canterberry. Sometimes I don't think you realize how condescending you sound. Like I'm only capable of two-syllable words."

"Vignette *is* a two-syllable word," I put in.

Griggs counted on her fingers before snapping, "I wasn't counting syllables literally. I was counting them figuratively."

I looked up at Nan. "That's how I do math. Explains my low grades."

Nan grunted at me before turning on Griggs. "It's not the fact that it's a vignette that concerns me," she said. "It's the fact that you, Dorigen Griggs, obviously had a hand in it."

Griggs grunted as she scanned the page. "There's Oswald's signature," she said, pointing to the bottom right-hand corner. "You need to give credit where credit is due."

"Oh, I'll do that all right, Dorigen Griggs. In fact, that's why I'm here now. He may have signed it, but you helped hold the pen."

I gasped and looked back down at the strip. Nan was right. Although I had my usual seasonal head—in this case it was a bookmark—from the way Oswald Elliot drew it, he'd either been a fly on the wall or he'd had a spy. A mole.

Griggs bit her lip. "What gave me away?"

"For starters, Oswald Elliot has never stepped foot through my front door, and as you can see, my living room is a bit too detailed to be guesswork. I'm speechless, Dorigen. You came into my home, invaded my privacy and, unbeknownst to me, revealed an intimate moment for all of Happy Valley to see."

"You don't seem speechless to me," Griggs fired back.

"That's nothing," I said, reaching over and fishing around in Griggs' apron pocket. Before she could stop me, I pulled out the strip Griggs had shown me earlier.

Nan snatched the paper out of my hand. "What's this?"

Griggs turned tomato red. "Nothing. Celia's just trying to cause trouble."

"I'll be the judge of that," Nan said, adding the strip to the fray. Nan read the same words that Griggs had read just a couple of days earlier, except when Nan read them it sounded so much worse. "*Despite her lowly status, Celia Canterberry manages to make one meagre friend. One daring child willing to forgo public scrutiny and face the withering looks of her countrymen. And this friend? Who could she be? None other than the steadfast Archibald Quigley, a scabby-kneed foundling that clings faithfully to Celia's side.*"

When she finished, Nan crumpled the strip. "What the hell, Dorigen?"

"Yeah," I said, picking up where Nan left off. "What kind of bullshit is this?"

Without taking her eyes off Griggs, Nan deftly cuffed me on the back of the head before I had a chance to duck.

Griggs slumped in her chair. "I didn't have a choice. Oswald Elliot was curled up in a corner somewhere, licking his wounds. He said he can't possibly go on now that Caroline Dobbs, his comic strip muse, has set her cap for Doctor Whitford. And to top it off, Mayor Forde threatened to get some outsider to step in, so I said I'd do it for free."

The life went out of her lazy eye as her ambitious one picked up the slack and did its best to carry on. "I tried to portray Celia in a respectful manner. She looks like a normal little girl; some might even say pretty. She and Archibald couldn't be sweeter."

"It's Eugenia that looks like a troll," Griggs went on. "Swallowing squirming children as if they were already dead. Have you ever heard of such a thing? Enid Whitford just about had a bird when she saw it. First time in history that the Happy Valley Journal had two printings, trying to keep up with all the copies that woman bought. Would have done another run if they hadn't run out of newsprint. It was only luck that I liberated my ten copies. Slipped them out of the burning barrel when Enid went to her garage to fetch a jerry can of gasoline. She even threatened to pull the Happy Valley Drugstore advertisements from the paper. That was, until she was offered a column of her own. *Titans in Transition.* The title was my idea. I told Enid it was a peace offering, to make up for any harm I might have done. I don't know what the hell it's supposed to mean, and it doesn't make up for the strip, but TIT is such an appropriate acronym."

Nan straightened the crumpled ball of newsprint, and the three of us re-examined the strip. She gave a curt nod. "It's still a betrayal."

"Maybe so," said Griggs. "But it was done with love."

Nan couldn't deny that. She ran a finger around the frame containing Archibald and me.

"Mayor Forde called it a debacle," Griggs went on. "Said I'm no longer allowed to have free reign; I can only advise. Hence the vignette. At the moment, it's all Oswald is capable of."

The three of us examined Oswald Elliot's latest creation.

"It's not so bad," I said, rubbing the back of my head. "Kind of has a Norman Rockwell feel to it."

"Norman Rockwell, my Aunt Fanny!" Nan snapped. "We look like a bunch of lunatics."

As Oswald had drawn it, Nan was in the middle of her chesterfield reading *Sense and Sensibility*, with Griggs and me snuggled in, one on either side. Next to Griggs was Captain Ahab, wearing his best peg leg and looking particularly dapper. Queequeg was draped over the back of the chesterfield like a swimsuit model. The only thing that might cause concern was Anna Karenina. She was a little worse for wear, crawling down the hallway, all ripped lace and smudge marks, dragging a gunny sack full of rotting potatoes. To my mind, it was fairly realistic. The way I would have drawn it if given a chance. Underneath, in bold print, it read, *Reading soothes all souls, living and imaginary*.

Nan rubbed an arthritic knuckle. "I can't count the times Enid Whitford snickered today. 'Always wondered what you did in your spare time,' she said. 'Your family is a regular sideshow. I'm surprised Tommy Hunter hasn't dialed you up; put you on stage alongside The Rhythm Pals.' And the icing on the cake— she cut out that little vignette and hung it on the bulletin board at the back of the store."

"She's just trying to get even," Griggs said. "She told Mayor Forde that you and I cooked up the Eugenia strip together. Said I wasn't smart enough to do it on my own."

Nan reached over and placed a hand on Griggs'. "I'm so sorry, Dorigen. I didn't know."

"I'm used to it."

"With that Whitford woman, if it's not one thing it's something else." Nan's nostrils flared. "First she insults you, then that goddamned woman asked me what I keep in my cellar."

There was a long silence, and I didn't know where to put myself. It was as if someone had seen Nan naked.

Griggs brought a hand to her mouth. "Oh Molly! What did you say?"

"Not a goddamn thing."

That's when I slipped out of Griggs' kitchen and headed for home. I wanted to be prepared. Nan was going to need at least two aspirins tonight.

9

Walter Douglas was waiting on Nan's doorstep when I rounded the corner. I did a quick scan for his cat, Tiberius, but that mangy beast was nowhere to be seen—which was a relief. Even though I claimed we were friends, that cat put the fear of God into almost everyone he came across. Especially Griggs. He'd crouch underneath her wooden step and swipe at the back of her legs whenever he had a chance. For the two of them, it was hate at first sight. It could have been her shifty eyes, or the thought that if she could get her hands on him, he'd land up alongside her husband, stuffed and fluffed with a warm bowl of milk as compensation.

As for Walter Douglas, he was wringing his hands and looking extra lost. I sat down beside him. He'd been sweet on Nan before the war. Griggs told me all about it. He'd bring Nan wildflowers and read her poetry. Everyone in Happy Valley was sure they'd marry, but when Walter Douglas got back from overseas, he was what Doc Marley called 'altered.' Griggs said he wasn't fit to marry anyone after that. Not even Nan.

"A crack in the teacup?" I asked.

He nodded, and slipped his hand over mine.

These were his and Nan's code words, the only ones needed. A crack in the teacup was a line from one of their favourite poems. *And the crack in the teacup opens a lane to the land of the dead.* Apparently, during the war, Walter Douglas' teacup cracked, and he'd been walking on a skeleton-riddled goat path ever since.

When Nan finally meandered home, the wind had kicked up. My teeth were chattering, and even with Walter's hands covering mine, my fingers were fish-belly blue. "What on earth?" she said, when she caught sight of us sitting on the cold step.

Walter Douglas stiffened, and I squeezed his hand. "You told me not to let anyone in the house when you're not home. And it would be rude to leave Mr. Douglas outside all by himself." That was true. Ever since my should-have-been parents snuck in to rob Nan, she'd insisted that no one was to come into the house unless she was home. "Not even Griggs?" I had complained.

Nan had snorted. "Especially Mrs. Griggs. It's hard enough to keep one step ahead of that woman without you letting the fox into the henhouse."

But now, seeing Walter and me turning into popsicles, I could tell she was rethinking one of her demands.

"Well, let's get you two inside before you catch your deaths." Nan herded us through the door. "I swear, some days..." She never finished the thought. She was too busy hanging up coats before rooting around in the refrigerator. "I bet you're hungry, Walter. You look like you're wasting away."

Walter's head bobbed almost imperceptibly, but Nan didn't notice. She wasn't even looking. "Do you mind having leftovers from Sunday dinner?"

This time, Walter shook his head.

"Good." She heated gravy in a frying pan and added slices of roast beef. The boiled potatoes she sliced and fried with butter and onions. Then she sprinkled the inside of a brown paper bag with droplets of water, dropped in the Yorkshire puddings and tossed the whole kit and caboodle into the warm oven. She treated all her day-old bread that way. Said it was almost the same as fresh baked. She was in the midst of her preparations when she turned to Walter. "Have you come about the storm windows?"

He nodded and took a seat at the chrome table. I took the seat beside him and stared up into his face. This was the first time I could remember Walter Douglas eating with us. Nan took food over to his house, and she ate with him at church picnics, and under the big tree at the fowl supper, but he'd never eaten at her own kitchen table.

"Well, don't just sit there," Nan scolded, as she bustled around the kitchen. Walter Douglas went to stand and Nan snapped her tongue. "Not you, Walter. I was talking to lazy bones."

I didn't budge. Nan knew my aversion to name calling. It was uncouth, reducing folks to the lowest common denominator. Except, that is, when it came to Timmy *Crybaby-Head*—but that was more of a description. I wrinkled my brow. I did call Griggs *Old Lady Griggs* and, more recently, Miss Dobbs *Bluebird Girl*. And I called my parents my *should-have-beens*. Hmmm, I guess the aversion only applied to me.

"Celia," she snapped. "The table needs to be set. You know the drill. Plates, cups, knives, and forks. Don't just sit there, get moving."

I pushed back my chair. I hated setting the table. Nan made it sound easy, like anybody with half a brain could do it, but that's where she was wrong. The extras always got me. Like what kind of pickles to use: bread and butter, dill, or beet? Or did she want dinner rolls or bread? I usually guessed at those things, half the time getting it wrong. The whole thing seemed like a waste of time. "Walter can help, if he wants," I said.

Nan turned on her heel so fast she was a blur. "Walter can help? Is that how I raised you? The first time he's sat down at my table for years, and you want to put him to work?"

I wanted to nod, but Nan's tone told me not to. "Only if he wants to," I said, trying to sound diplomatic. "I don't want him to feel left out."

"The only one that's going to feel left out is you! Another word from you, Miss Swiss, and you'll be eating up in your room. Alone."

Sometimes Nan didn't have a clue. The thought of eating in my room made me light up inside. Captain Ahab would jump for joy. Peg leg or not, he'd swing me in his arms and call me clever. After that, we'd arm wrestle to see who'd have to eat the gristle. The only thing that gave me pause was Walter Douglas. It would be a shame to abandon him on our first official sit-down dinner. Leave him and Nan alone to their silent chewing. USSE, Uninterrupted Sustained Silent Eating. What could be worse than that? But then again, this opportunity might only knock once.

Nan must have read my mind, because she added, "On second thought, a better place might be with Anna Karenina in the cellar."

I gasped. Anna Karenina was fine in the garden, where I could wear my Russian rubber boots. There I could be her quite easily, fussing about her delicate hands, expressing her disdain for multi-legged creatures, as well as hard work and breathing peasant air. But eating with her, as her, would be unacceptable. "She insists on white gloves and starched linens," I reminded Nan.

"She'll get over it."

"The lighting in the cellar makes her skin sallow, and

Countess Vronsky would never let her live it down. And that will only make Anna get her back up. Vronsky is worse than Mrs. Whitford, and you know what *she's* like."

Nan grunted, but I had made my point.

That's why I had no choice but to set the table in protest, but not so much of a protest that it would rile Nan. Let her think I was being careless in the excitement of having an evening guest. First, the somewhat muted thunder of the melamine plates; then, the hollow thunks of the Tupperware cups. The cutlery was another story. It clattered without much encouragement. The trick was to have it clatter a little more than usual, but not enough for Nan to turn on me. I'd become adept at that. I practiced when Nan was mowing the yard or shoveling snow.

Nan surveyed the table. "You forgot the napkins," was all she said. Not *nice job*, or *couldn't have done better myself*. I wanted to tell her that the napkins would have to be washed and ironed, and considering her busy schedule, it was unadvisable —we could use our sleeves, like I usually did when she wasn't looking. But Nan seemed to want to make things extra special for our guest. Like he was someone extraordinary, like our visit might get written about in Happy Valley's "Titans in Transition" column, Mrs. Whitford's new opinion piece focussing on the PIS Ladies and their most treasured friends. Besides, Walter Douglas wouldn't notice a napkin if it hit him in the face. Probably never even used one before. In fact, I bet he wouldn't even care if I ate with my hands. That's how much of a gentleman he was. But there was no use telling Nan that. She'd have me down in the cellar before I could say Jack Robinson, and not just for the duration of the meal.

Nan bowed her head, but instead of saying *For what we are about to receive, may the Lord make us truly thankful*, like she usually did, the way any normal person would, she hesitated.

She sat there stalk still while the food cooled. I wanted to reach out and give her a shake, tell her to get a move on. The one and only time a man comes over for supper and she loses her mind! When she finally got around to saying the blessing, it wasn't like any blessing I'd heard before.

"Come live with me, and be my love, and we will all the pleasures prove that hills and valleys, dales and field, woods and craggy moun- tains yield...."

I wanted to roll my eyes, look at Walter Douglas, and say, *I don't know why she's being extra fancy this time.* But the coward in me prevailed.

"And we will sit upon the rocks, and see the shepherd feed their flocks, by shallow rivers, to whose falls melodious birds sing madri- gals," she continued. *"And I will make thee beds of roses, and a thousand fragrant posies: a cap of flowers, and a kittle embroider'd all with leaves of myrtle..."*

I was drooling now, wasting away for food I wasn't even sure I was going to like. By the time Nan was through her flowery exaltation, all my taste buds would probably be dead. I wanted to stand up and shout, *Use your Agnes Obermeyer voice.* At least that way it would be entertaining. The only problem was, Nan didn't have an Agnes Obermeyer voice. Where was Griggs when I needed her? She did the best Agnes Obermeyer in the whole county.

When I snuck a peek at Walter Douglas, his cheeks were burning like a red-hot poker, and I couldn't tell if it was out of anger or frustration. No wonder he never came over for supper. Having to listen to an old woman's lamentations just to get a few mouthfuls of lukewarm food couldn't be worth it.

"A gown made of the finest wool, which from our pretty lambs we pull, fair-lined slippers for the cold, with buckles of the purest gold..."

I groaned as I laid my head on the table, but Nan didn't even notice. She was mid-verse. *"A belt of straw and ivy buds with coral clasps and amber studs: and if these pleasures may thee move, Come live with me, and be my love."*

I wanted to pat Walter Douglas on the hand and say, *It's usually not this bad. We could play a hand of kings in the corner with all the time she's wasting.*

Nan didn't make any sense to me. It was times like this I missed Griggs. No matter who pulled up a chair, her grace was practical and to the point. *Cut the meat, let's eat.* So many things to admire about that woman.

"The shepherd swains shall dance and sing for thy delight each May-morning: If these delights thy mind may move, then live with me, and be my love."

By the time Nan passed the first bowl, she didn't even need a pot holder. I saw the judgement fill Walter Douglas' eyes, but like a good sport he held his tongue and filled his plate. He took extra big helpings, as if he weren't aware that I was next in line. There was hardly anything left when the bowls came back around to Nan. But she didn't seem to mind, politely nibbling on a scrap of beef dribbled in left-over gravy.

I almost felt sorry for her, until I remembered her telling Griggs that she had an extra five pounds she was struggling to shed. Maybe having Walter Douglas over for supper was part of her weight loss plan.

As we ate, the only sound was knives and forks scraping across Nan's plates, accompanied by the sound of our tumblers being lifted and set back down on the table. The whole time, Nan and Walter Douglas exchanged glances. Nan glanced when Walter looked away, and Walter glanced while Nan looked down. They were like two broken-winged song birds.

So why was I the one who felt like regurgitating?

I puffed out my cheeks. This was almost as bad as the day I caught Timmy Crybaby-Head mooning over Archibald Quigley, my once-upon-a-time best friend. He didn't moon over her when she was still speaking to him. He took her for granted then, as if she'd always be around. I kind of did the same thing, the taking for granted part, but not as much as him. It wasn't until she glued herself to Eugenia Whitford that he became a lot aware, and me a little bit aware, that she was a living, breathing thing.

Of course, Timmy denied it. He said he wasn't mooning. That he only looked that way when he was concentrating or peeing. But I'd been paying attention. The only person in class he seemed to concentrate on was Archibald Quigley. He mostly concentrated on the back of her head, because she usually refused to turn around and look at him, even when he loudly whispered her name or beaned a balled-up piece of paper at her. Nan and Walter Douglas were long past the whispering and paper throwing stage. They were too busy with their eyes ducking and weaving.

Nan cleared her throat. "The storm windows are in the shed, where you put them last spring." She said it as if it were an apology. "I haven't had time to drag them out and give them a wash." She sighed. "But to tell you the truth, I haven't wanted to. The weather's been so lovely that the thought of taking the screens down seems counterintuitive. That being said, now that nights are getting so cold, I don't think I have a choice." She crossed her knife and fork over her plate. "I'll miss my fresh air, though. Reminds me of younger days."

Walter nodded, but didn't say anything. And I wondered how long it'd been since the air had smelled fresh to him.

10

I slid my desk snug beside Timmy Crybaby-Head's when a thought popped into my head. "Hey Timmy," I said.

He didn't hey me back.

"Okay, let's get this straight, Crybaby-Head. When I 'hey you' it's only polite to 'hey me' back." I was using Griggs' latest advice from Dale Carnegie's book, *How to Win Friends and Influence People*. That was, to use a person's name, as it is the sweetest, most important sound to them.

"I don't want to 'hey you,'" he said, through lips as tight as a sideshow ventriloquist's. "I don't want to sit next to you. I don't want to be your partner."

I smiled. "Well, at least that's a start. Now we're talking."

Timmy stuck out his tongue as Miss Dobbs made her way to the front of the room. "Class," she said. "As I've said before, we need to make sure we're ready for the Halloween Spooktacular." She rose on her toes at the excitement of the event. "And as I've already told you, we are the chosen class. Not the irritating Grade Threes, or the obnoxious Grade Fours, but the humble Grade Twos." She did a slight bow. "Does anyone remember this year's theme?"

Loads of kids put up their hand, but the only one Miss Dobbs had eyes for was Eugenia's. "Yes, my dear?"

"Who are the people in *my* neighbourhood?"

"If only we could be so lucky. Showcasing you would ensure that the project would be a success, but alas we have to include the rest of the class. Parents these days are so fussy, always complaining. *Where was little Johnny?* and *Wasn't Sally the cutest?*" She paused and looked directly at Sally Shephard. "Don't worry, your mother would never say that about you. Now where was I? Oh yes, it's enough to make me scream." She rolled her eyes. "As if I care about the drivel most of you spout."

I wanted to put up my hand and say, *You're preaching to the choir, sister*, but thought better of it. I was part of the spouting drivel she didn't care about.

"Now let's get one thing straight. None of you are to show up in Halloween garb. And that includes you, Celia Canterberry. No one wants to see a wart-covered witch talk about some illiterate gas jockey. Or a hump-backed vampire drone on about an uncle who pounds fence posts or cleans ditches on his days off. We want to elevate the experience. Wake up the people of this backwater to a different way of being incongruous."

I raised my hand. "I don't think *being incongruous* is the right phrase."

"Did I ask you, Celia Canterberry?" Miss Dobbs' eyes bore into me.

"Nope, but I still don't think it's right. Even Old Lady Griggs could tell you that. The phrase you're looking for is not *being incongruous*. Nan would call it a rookie mistake, using large words beyond your grasp. But I have to admit I admire you for trying." I scratched my chin. "I think *behaving with more comportment* would work better. Sounds educated, like you read books in your spare time."

Miss Dobbs didn't take kindly to my advice. "In the second

grade and you think you know everything. For your information, the English language is fluid. Always changing, evolving." Her gaze burned into me as she clomped over to the bookshelf and took down the dictionary. The spine cracked as she flipped it open. "What a word means one day may not be what it means the next." She flipped some more, her lips moving as she read. There was a long pause before she cleared her throat. "As I was saying before Celia rudely interrupted me, we need to show this backwater a new way of comportment. That's why, unlike other years, we're going to forgo the usual shenanigans. Hence —which is the right word, Celia Canterberry, so don't bother putting up your hand—the lack of Halloween regalia. Or, for those of you who lack a strong vocabulary, *costumes*."

The class was deathly quiet as Miss Dobbs' words sunk in. No costumes, no Halloween regalia, and, worst of all, no shenanigans. Never in my life had I thought about giving up those wonderful things. I'd been looking forward to this year's shenanigans ever since I'd wiped off last year's Halloween makeup. As a whole, the class stifled a sob.

Sally Shephard always went as the wolfman. It was her way of preparing the rest of us for things to come. Timmy Crybaby-Head liked to be unpredictable. One year he went as a snail, and another as a garden slug, but my favourite was when he came as an octopus; he was anything that would leave a slimy trail. That way, no one was sure what they were stepping in. But most of all, I'd miss Farmer Hempel. Last year he came as a real live mummy. Ripped up his wife's favourite bedsheets when she was in the bath.

He'd lumbered around, a low growl grumbling in the back of his throat, scaring anyone who ventured too close. He didn't even notice his bandages getting entangled until he tripped right into the bobbing-for-apples barrel. The splash doused one of Mrs. Whitford's owl children, causing her to dissolve on the spot. It was like watching a circus sideshow. Mrs. Whitford grabbed Farmer Hempel by the scruff of the neck and dunked his head deep into the barrel. All the while, her daughter cried bloody murder.

The only one to comfort the poor little sot was Old Lady Griggs, and I wasn't sure she was much comfort at all. Griggs pulled a never-ending supply of used Kleenex from under her brassiere strap and tossed them at the girl. The hard bits binged off her forehead like bits of hail. When asked about it later, Griggs said she couldn't just stand by and do nothing. It wouldn't be Christian.

It took three men to drag Mrs. Whitford off Farmer Hempel, and by the time he drew his next breath, he was half drowned. His wife's best sheet hung in loops around his neck, revealing his ashen face. It was tough to be a farmer. We all clapped our appreciation as if the fiasco had been for entertainment purposes, and not because Mrs. Whitford, a pharmacist's wife, had gotten the best of him.

And now Miss Dobbs was asking us to give all this up. Said that we needed to show the town a new way of comportment. Comportment! If she had it her way, we'd all be as prissy as Eugenia Whitford. Eugenia Whitford! There was no joy in that.

"It bears repeating," Miss Dobbs went on, taking our stunned silence for rapt enthusiasm, "for those of you that have forgotten, that the theme is *Who are the People in our Neighbourhood*? I wouldn't have to repeat myself so often if some of your families hadn't spent such an inordinate amount of time fishing from the same pond." She looked directly at Billy Billboson. "Would it have killed your mother to learn to spell a new last name? And Sally, wouldn't you like at least two sets of grandparents?"

Miss Dobbs' tone softened as her gaze hovered over Eugenia. "But thank God none of these shortcomings have been visited on the Whitfords. They have been stalwart in their devotion to purity. So, after all these years of teaching, it goes without saying that Eugenia is a breath of fresh air. She's the only pupil who's like a daughter to me. Birds of a feather as they say. I have birthing pains every time I think of her."

I grunted. "I'll agree with you there, she's a pain in the ass, all right." But Miss Dobbs didn't hear me. She was too busy having a moment with Eugenia.

"Considering that Eugenia has so expertly divided you into groups," she droned on, "now it's up to you to decide which neighbourhood people you'll pick. Each group will have to discuss two different members of our community. I'll give you ten minutes to decide, and then I'll randomly call each group to the front where they can tell the class the subject of their presentation. Once a neighbourhood person is claimed, no one else will be able to talk about them. That way there won't be any repetition and we are less likely to bore the audience."

Billy Billboson raised his hand. "What's repetition?"

"Billy, Billy, Billy." Miss Dobbs shook her head. "You'd think by second grade you'd know the meaning of a simple word like that. Repetition is when something is repeated. Like when an uncle marries a niece. Or when I said Billy, Billy, Billy. One Billy would have been enough. Three Billys were just to let you know how irritated I am." She scanned the room. "Any other stupid questions?"

Surprisingly, there weren't any.

"Good. Let's get started."

Everyone began whispering and making lists, afraid if they were overheard someone might steal their neighbourhood person. Everyone, that is, except me and Crybaby-Head. Timmy had turned his back and stuck his fingers in his ears. To get his attention, I tapped him on the shoulder. When that didn't work, I flicked him on the head until my fingers got sore. Finally

I gave up. With his attitude, what was the use of even trying? So, I laid my head on my desk and took a nap.

The next thing I knew, Miss Dobbs was clapping her hands. "Settle down, class. It's time to hear which two neighbourhood people each of your groups have chosen. And to make things fair, I'll close my eyes." Eyes clamped shut, Miss Dobbs made a humming sound as her sharp finger made circles in the air. When it stopped, it was pointing straight at Eugenia. Miss Dobbs opened her eyes and tried to look shocked. "Well," she said, "isn't that a coincidence."

The class groaned.

I grabbed Timmy's arm and used his sleeve to wipe the pool of drool from my desk. "That's not a coincidence, that's cheating," I said. "Eugenia sits in the front row, same desk since she moved here. The one you made Archibald vacate."

"My eyes were closed," Miss Dobbs said, her lips thinning.

"Prove it. Prove it wasn't cheating. Close your eyes and we'll all change desks. See who you pick first then."

"Oh, I don't think that's necessary."

Eugenia agreed, and at the thought of repeating the process she burst into tears. "But I need to go first. I always go first."

"You can still go first," I said. "If she picks you again. At least then it will be a real coincidence."

Miss Dobbs slapped her yardstick on the side of her leg. "The only one who thinks it's cheating is you, Celia Canterberry. Isn't that right, class?"

Everyone shifted in their seats and looked at their fellow classmates. "Can we at least try?" Sally Shephard asked, twitching her burgeoning moustache.

"It would make us all feel better," Billy Billboson chimed in.

"Very well then, for the sake of fairness, I'll choose again." Miss Dobbs closed her eyes, counting to ten. Everyone switched seats, but nobody would take Timmy Crybaby-Head's, afraid of wood rot. Miss Dobbs finished her counting, and after a little peeking she pointed straight at Eugenia. "Well, it was meant to be!" she crowed.

Eugenia sprang from her seat before anyone could protest, grabbed Archibald, and dragged her to the front of the classroom. There she blurted out, "The people in my neighbourhood will be a doctor, like my dad, and a pharmacist, like my uncle."

Miss Dobbs looked like she was going to cry, as if all her hopes and dreams had been dashed to the ground and she didn't even have a dustpan to collect them in. But before she could completely dissolve, Eugenia gazed up at her like she was the Madonna in the Christmas pageant. "And a teacher, just like Miss Dobbs."

"She picked three," I protested. "You let her go first and she can't even count."

"She can pick as many as she likes. Unlike the rest of you, Eugenia is an overachiever." Miss Dobbs stifled a joyous sob before looking down and combing her fingers through Eugenia's looping pigtails. "Oh, Eugenia, I couldn't be more pleased." Her forehead furrowed. "But what is Archibald going to talk about? After all, it is a group project."

"She'll do all the parts I don't want to. Like taking notes and fetching snacks." She jabbed Archibald in the ribs. "Isn't that right, partner?"

Archibald gave a dutiful nod.

I threw up in my mouth a little bit.

Miss Dobbs seemed satisfied with this and wrote their three professions on the board. She reminded the class that there would be no doubling up. "Children can prattle on and on about the most mundane things. God knows I have to listen to it all day. And if I have to spend an entire evening listening to the same drivel, I'll lose my mind." She closed her eyes and picked the Bobbsey twins. They weren't real twins—they weren't even related—but they were both so bland that I never remembered their real names. Most days I didn't even remember that they were in my class. The unremarkable pair picked a tailor (Mr. Murry, from Murry's Haberdashery), and a farmer—Farmer Hempel.

Sally Shephard and Billy Billboson picked a baker (Mrs. Jasmine, who owned the bakery), and an ambulance driver— Ned. You get the picture. As Miss Dobbs' sneaky pointing wound its way around the classroom, there was hardly a choice left. Lenard and Bartholomew picked Mayor Forde and his secretary, Agnes Obermeyer. To me, that was the most disappointing pick of all. I didn't think anyone would pick Mayor Forde, not when Griggs always said he was the longest-running political pariah ever elected to office.

I raised my hand. "If Lenard is going to talk about Mayor Forde, can Timmy and me talk about his belly button rodent?"

Miss Dobbs clip-clopped to my desk in record time. "Who has a belly button rodent?" She looked more annoyed than usual.

"Mayor Forde." It was hard not to add *Occam's razor* to my reply, but Miss Dobbs had forbidden me from using it as my go-to response. Besides, since Archibald dumped me, nothing made sense anymore, no matter how much I Occam razored it. I cleared my throat and envisioned myself standing in front of a throng of spellbound Happy Valleyans, all hanging on my every word. "Little known fact. Mayor Forde, being a man of immensity, has lost the ability to reach every itch." I looked up at Miss Dobbs. So far, so good. She wasn't interrupting or wildly swinging the yardstick.

"Thus, as any great leader who has taken their place in the annals of history, he has enlisted the help of another species. Like Alexander the Great's horse, Bucephalus, or the she-wolf who suckled Romulus and Remus. Mayor Forde's yet to be named companion, living deep in the cavernous depths of his navel, is as elusive as the Loch Ness Monster, although many a child has gawked at that gaping hole—exposed by a shirt pulled taut between straining buttons—in hopes of a sighting."

Miss Dobbs was silent for a long time. I smiled smugly at the back of Archibald's head. She wasn't the only one who could sound like an encyclopedia.

"Those aren't real people," Miss Dobbs finally said.

"Tell Romulus that," I said, as the bell announced the end of the school day.

11

iss Dobbs was left digesting my spiel as I skipped past her and out of the classroom. She didn't even get a chance to cow-kick me. It was hard not to feel particularly pleased with myself, but feeling particularly pleased didn't last long. Archibald was waiting for Eugenia in the hallway, the way she used to wait for me.

"Don't forget your lunch pail, Archibald," Eugenia said. "And your mittens. It's getting cold out."

My eyes narrowed. Those were the words I used to say. "Copycat," I huffed under my breath.

"Did Seasonal-Head say something?" Eugenia swung around, her eyes large with wonder.

"Don't call her that." Archibald's voice came out as a whisper.

My heart stilled.

"Call her what? Seasonal-Head? Everyone calls her that."

"No they don't. You do."

"Well, everyone that counts does." Eugenia's laser-beamed gaze burned right into me as she grabbed Archibald's hand and gave her arm an extra hard swing.

My gaze laser-beamed back, but that's all I could do. I had no one's arm to swing. No one to be my faithful sidekick. Unless... I scanned the hallway. Sally Shephard was down by the water fountain. I could run down and grab her hand, but by the time I'd dragged her back Eugenia and Archibald would be long gone. Billy Billboson was a little closer, but considering all the Brylcreem he used keeping Larry, Moe and Curly under control, his hands would be too slippery to get a tight grip.

That's when Timmy Crybaby-Head slipped out of the classroom. He stopped short when he caught sight of Eugenia and I, his eyes flicking from one to the other. I wanted to scream, *I'm the one who should terrify you most; she's just an interloper*, but I didn't have to. He had made his decision; I saw it in his eyes. Taking a running start, he tried to zoom past me, avoiding Eugenia altogether. He ran so fast I had to clothes-line him. As Timmy choked, trying to catch his breath, I grabbed his hand and gave it a hard swing. For his part, Timmy made a gallant effort to screech his protest, but due to his crushed larynx, he couldn't make a sound. I almost felt sorry for him.

Eugenia sniffed. "On second thought, maybe you're right, Archibald. Maybe I shouldn't call her Seasonal-Head. It sounds too festive, and now that she has a boyfriend it would be rude to ignore him." She tapped a finger to her chin. "Perhaps Thing 1 and Thing 2 would work better. Has a nice ring to it."

Archibald didn't say anything; she just stood there with an empty look. I wanted her to scream, spit, stomp her feet. I wanted her to fling herself at Eugenia, ripping at her hair so fiercely that it would take five teachers to pry her off. I'd be proud of her then. I'd even slip my hand into hers as Miss Dobbs dragged her down the hall to the principal's office. But what I wanted didn't seem to matter to Archibald. Once again I was left to defend myself. "He's not my boyfriend," I said, dropping Timmy's hand. To press the point, I slugged Timmy as hard as I could in the shoulder he was favouring.

Eugenia narrowed her eyes. "Did Thing 1 say something? I couldn't hear her with all of Thing 2's whimpering."

"Shut up."

"You shut up."

I was about to call her a copycat, but it would have been a waste of time. Eugenia would never let me have the last word. Besides, with all Timmy's caterwauling, she'd have never heard my witty retort. He sounded like a cat in heat, and he was just revving up. So much so it sent most of the kids scurrying out the school door. All but Sally Shephard and Billy Billboson, that is. They edged towards us, eyes fixed on Timmy, who'd dropped to the floor and was foaming at the mouth. I saw Sally lean over and whisper something in Billy's ear. He nodded as he gave a comforting pat to Larry, Moe and Curly. Sally, although she tried to hide it behind her burgeoning moustache, seemed particularly impressed. Being from a long line of former circus performers, Sally knew a good sideshow when she saw one.

Timmy's incoherent wailing morphed into words. "Make it stop, make it stop."

I placed my hands on my knees before hollering back, "Make what stop?"

Timmy screamed louder, as if my voice burned his eardrums. His heels dug into the tiles so hard he began to pinwheel himself in a lopsided circle. It was mesmerizing. Timmy was becoming the Pied Piper of the Happy Valley School for Reluctant Children. Kids that had already left the school were coming back, and to tell you the truth, I never saw it coming. For a second I admired him. Even so, I had to get control of the situation, because it would be only a matter of time before a teacher pulled themselves away from their end-of-day smoke and looked for the source of the inconvenience. If the past was any indication, what caused the inconvenience would most assuredly be attributed to me.

"Stop what?" I repeated.

Timmy pinwheeled harder. To get his attention, I did the only reasonable thing I could think of. I wound up, knowing a good kick would make him rethink the scene he was making. But instead of nailing him in the shin I'd aimed for, I inadvertently punted him in his injured shoulder. That only made things worse. If Timmy sounded like a cat in heat before, now he sounded like one being torn limb from limb.

Eugenia swung Archibald's arm as sweetly as if they were at a Sunday picnic. "Like I said before, Thing 1 and Thing 2." As soon as the words were out of her mouth, she turned on her heel, dragging Archibald along behind her.

It was only when Miss Dobbs yanked on my earlobe that my attention turned back to Timmy.

"What's wrong with him?"

I shrugged. Timmy still hadn't exhausted himself, although his pinwheeling had slowed. I almost felt sorry for Miss Dobbs. She didn't know how to process childhood misery that she hadn't inflicted herself.

"Do something about it," she snapped.

I bent down over Timmy, not sure what to do. Kicking him had proved ineffectual, and punching would most likely be counterproductive. I glanced from Sally to Billy; they shrugged a response. It galled me to have to comfort someone who crumbled at a real good arm swing. So I said the only thing that made sense. "You're a non-speaking tree."

Timmy's pinwheeling stopped and his eyes widened, recognizing the reference to our long-ago shenanigans.

"That's right," I said, glancing up at Miss Dobbs. "And you know what happens to non-speaking trees that forget they don't have vocal cords?"

Timmy looked up at me, horrified. "They get thrown in a fire," he mouthed.

I wanted to tell him not to look at me that way; that it was J.R.R. Tolkien who made the rules, not me. Instead, I replied, "Exactly."

Miss Dobbs snorted. She didn't seem to hear the threat, or if she did, she didn't care. Without giving Timmy a second glance, she clip-clopped back into her classroom. I blew out my cheeks. That was a close call. Bringing up the day that Archibald, Timmy, and me let the air out of Miss Dobbs' tires was a risk. Miss Dobbs had blamed Oswald Elliot, thinking it was a romantic gesture on his part. She'd expected him to step out from the shadows and rescue her. Never once did it occur to her that we were playing Tom Sawyer. Archibald, with her tight little ways was, of course, Tom, while I was an entirely believable Huckleberry Finn. With all the good roles taken, Timmy had been relegated to the part of a non-speaking tree. The part suited him, as it allowed Archibald and me to sleep peacefully. A non-speaking tree could never tell on us or give us away, no matter how much it was tempted to. Besides, it would go against the undeclared rules of make-believe.

By the time I made it halfway back to Nan's house, Timmy and me were almost friends. It all started with me offering Timmy a hand. He accepted without thinking and allowed me to help him to his feet. When it dawned on him what he had done, it was too late. We already had an uneasy truce.

"Want to walk me home?" I asked.

"Not really."

"How about if I walk you home?"

He shrugged but didn't refuse. We'd walked most of the way to Timmy's house when I got an idea. Seeing a flicker of the old Archibald back at school must have inspired me before she dashed my hopes once more. As much as I swore I'd never play

Jane Eyre again, I was tempted to go back on my word. Timmy would make an unusual Helen.

"Want to play a game?" I asked Timmy, as we kicked pebbles down the sidewalk.

"What kind of game?"

"A pretend one," I said. Before he could protest, I added, "Except this time you don't have to be a non-speaking tree. You can be a real person."

"A real person?" A note of hope crept into his voice.

"Well, a real book person," I corrected myself.

Timmy bit at his lip, and I knew his little mind was churning it over.

"You can be the Scarlet Pimpernel. Doesn't that sound nice?"

"That doesn't sound like a person. That sounds like acne."

"It's not. It's the code name of Sir Percy Blakeney. He is one of the richest men in England. Everyone thinks he's kind of weak and foppish, but anyone who reads a lot knows that's code for bladder issues."

Timmy went white, and I knew he was ready to bolt. Pretending to be someone as misunderstood as the Scarlet Pimpernel would be like driving nails into his coffin. That's when I played my trump card. "But secretly, he rescues people from getting their heads chopped off."

Stopping short, Timmy gasped and brought a hand to his throat. After being recently clotheslined by yours truly, he had an intimate understanding.

"And," I went on, "he has a beautiful wife."

His eyes went as big as bottle caps. "That's not you, right?"

I bristled at his tone. "Yes, that's not me."

Timmy let out a sigh of relief. "Can her name be Archibald?"

He was losing the thread, but what could I expect? The only book character he'd ever been was a non-speaking tree. "That's not the way it works. You can't just pick names willy-nilly. Sir Percy's wife's name is Marguerite St. Just, but most people call her Lady Blakeney. And yes, Archibald can be Lady Blakeney." I wanted to add that it would serve her right, but some thoughts were best kept to myself.

Timmy chewed over my words for a while, then nodded. "And who are you going to be?"

I looked into the near distance and let the cool fall breeze tussle my hair. "Boudicca!"

12

The next time we had book club, Walter Douglas was putting on the storm windows. He had ambled over earlier in the day and started shifting the screens to the shed before replacing them with their winter counterparts. Griggs, who on her best day barely tolerated Walter Douglas, was coming out of her skin with all the banging. "How am I supposed to concentrate on the nuances with all this racket going on?" she asked, her purse swinging from her bent arm.

"You don't have to be here, Dorigen. Nobody asked you." Nan eyed the handbag. "Besides, it looks like you have other plans."

"The only plan I have is to look stylish. You should think about that sometimes. And I don't need to remind you that I don't have to be asked. With you I have an open-door policy. That's what happens when you're refrigerator friends."

"Refrigerator friends?"

"Yes. You know, the kind of friend who can look in your refrigerator and you don't have to worry about being judged."

"I've never looked in your refrigerator."

"And I've never judged you for it."

I sighed. Sometimes Griggs was right for all the wrong reasons. It wasn't Walter's banging that should have caused concern; that wouldn't stop me from concentrating on the story at hand. It was that I had an almost friend, one that wasn't Archibald. One that wasn't even a girl. Someone who was not only scared of his shadow, but peed on it. How was I going to tell Captain Ahab that? He still hadn't come to terms with Griggs putting her two cents in. "What would that lunatic know about anything?" he'd said, polishing his one good tooth. "Her husband has a stuffed nylon for a head."

Neither Nan nor Griggs noticed my discomfort. They were too busy rolling their eyes at one another and shaking the popcorn. By the time we made our way to the chesterfield, I wasn't sure I wanted to be at book club at all.

Nan settled down between Griggs and me and patted the book on her lap. "Where were we?"

"Mr. Dashwood," I said, getting my oar in before Griggs did. Just because I didn't want to be at book club didn't mean I was going to let Griggs one-up me. "He made his son promise to take care of his stepmother and sisters after he died."

"But," Griggs cut in, "his son is as useless as tits on a turkey, letting his wife lead him around by the nose. They'll be lucky if they get to keep their own teeth."

I nodded. "It's just like *The Giving Tree*. John and Fanny Dashwood want Mrs. Dashwood and his sisters to give up everything and act thrilled to do so. Except the good Dash-wood's aren't like *The Giving Tree*. They don't have any choices, and they aren't happy about it."

Nan looked pleased. "Very good, Celia."

"I said the very same thing," Griggs snorted. "The only difference was that I used teeth as the example instead of trees."

Nan ignored her and started reading. At first I thought

Griggs was going to sit there and listen with rapt interest, like I usually did. But it was not to be.

"*Devonshire!*" Nan read. "*Are you, indeed, going there? So far from hence! And to what part of it?*" She explained the situation. It *was within four miles northward of Exeter.*"

Griggs cleared her throat before proclaiming, "King Arthur's sword."

"King Arthur's *sword?*" Nan snapped. "What does that have to do with the price of rice in China?"

"You're not the only one who reads, Molly Canterberry. Everyone with even a smattering of book learning knows that Exeter is the name of King Arthur's sword."

Nan's jaw went slack. "*Excalibur.* That's the name of his sword."

"My mistake. I must be confusing it with his knife." She tapped the page to urge Nan to read on.

I sat in wonder. It was hard to believe, but Griggs aggravated Nan more than I did.

"*It is but a cottage,*" she continued, "*but I hope to see many of my friends in it. A room or two can easily be added; and if my friends find no difficulty in travelling so far to see me, I am sure I will find none in accommodating them.....*"

Walter Douglas provided the next interruption. He'd taken down the screen and was about to attach the storm window when he stopped to listen to Nan's reading. Balancing on the ladder by the window, propped open to catch what was left of the breeze, he hung on her every word.

Griggs was the first to notice. "He's staring," she said.

Nan looked up from the book. "Walter?"

He didn't say anything, just kept looking at Nan the way he did when they were stacking gunnysacks in the cellar.

"A crack in the teacup?" I asked.

"Not this time. This time it's companionship." Nan

motioned for Walter to come inside. "The windows can keep. Come join us."

He nodded, and before I knew it our little book club had sprouted another member.

Nan continued. *"Mr. John Dashwood told his mother again and again how exceedingly sorry he was that she had taken a house at such a distance from Norland as to prevent his being of any service to her in removing her furniture..."*

Nan read with more enthusiasm as soon as Walter joined the mix, and I thought it must have brought her back to her younger days when they used to read to each other under the shade of some majestic tree—words from all the books they read lingering in its branches. When she got to where Marianne Dashwood and her younger sister Margaret were taking a stroll, Nan's voice warmed as if plucking her own particular memory.

"They gaily ascended the downs, rejoicing in their own penetration at every glimpse of blue sky; and when they caught in their faces the animating gales of a high south-westerly wind, they pitied the fears which had prevented their mother and Elinor from sharing such delightful sensations..."

Around the time Nan read, *"They gaily ascended the downs,"* I spied Tiberius, Walter's mangy cat, slip as quiet as you like through the propped open window and under the chesterfield. I could have interrupted Nan and told her of the intruder, but we'd never had a cat in the house before, and the thought of snuggling up to him in the middle of the night thrilled me to no end. He might bring comfort to the sliver of a crack that was forming in my own little teacup.

The only problem was that Tiberius didn't snuggle. Walter, the only human he tolerated, was covered with scratches. Griggs said he was as wild as the west Texas wind, and for once I agreed with her. Still, there was always a possibility. Can't close the door on hope.

"They set off. Marianne had at first the advantage, but a false step brought her suddenly to the ground; and Margaret, unable to stop herself to assist her, was involuntarily hurried along, and reached the bottom in safety."

That's when Tiberius chose to rake his claws down the back of Griggs' leg. Griggs let out a bone-chilling shriek and catapulted herself off the chesterfield. My gaze swung to Walter. Griggs' caterwauling was sure to send almost anyone into hysterics, and considering his background, he was the most likely anyone I knew. Despite Walter's discomfort though, I changed my mind and was kind of pleased to be in book club. It was shifting my thoughts from my own dismal existence.

"Honestly, Dorigen," Nan said, as she slapped the book shut. "Do you really think that was necessary? The foolish girl just fell down a hill."

Griggs' eyes were wild, her lazy one flip-flopping while her ambitious one bore into Walter. "I told you he couldn't be trusted," she bellowed. "That he wasn't right in the head. If I had a gun—"

All the callisthenics Nan had been doing for the past few months were brought to bear on Griggs. If Griggs catapulted off the chesterfield, Nan rocketed. She clapped a hand over Griggs' mouth before Griggs had a chance to draw her next breath. And Griggs did what anyone with a half decent set of dentures would do. She bit her.

Nan yanked her pulsating finger from Griggs' maw. I knew what she wanted to say: *Son-of-a-bitch.* I could see it in her eyes. Instead, she grabbed the bowl of popcorn I was holding and dumped it on Griggs' head.

Griggs gulped as if she were a fish out of water. "If I'd known book club was going to be like this, I'd never have accepted your invitation."

"That would have saved me a perfectly good bowl of popcorn," Nan shot back.

I wanted to remind Nan that Griggs hadn't actually been invited, that she'd insinuated herself into our little gathering, but decided it was wiser to keep my mouth shut. To comfort myself, I stood on a pile of chesterfield cushions and plucked buttery flakes from Griggs' ruined curls.

The whole time Nan and Griggs were having it out, Walter stewed. He was as worked up as I'd ever seen him, mumbling "*a crack in the teacup*" over and over again. When Nan finally came to her senses and reached out to comfort him, he was pale and trembling.

"See what you've done, Dorigen," Nan hissed.

Griggs wiped a hand across the back of her leg and held it in the air. She shuddered at her bloody palm. "How am I going to explain this to Mr. Griggs? 'I was at a book club and things got carried away'? Even he won't believe that. Besides," she pointed at her legs, "these are my best hose. The only ones that aren't soaped up to stop the runs. I can't feel superior to all the other book club attendees in them now."

Nan's lips tightened. "We are the other book club attendees."

"Exactly. Need I say more?" She let out a long breath. "And if it weren't for that mangy cat, I wouldn't have had to say anything at all."

As if on cue, Tiberius crawled out from his hiding place to fling himself through the open window. I saw Nan's lip twitch, and I knew she'd be slipping him a can of tuna as soon as she got a chance.

No one spoke for a long time. Nan was steaming, Griggs was moaning, and Walter looked as if he'd been wacked about the head by Lizzie Borden, that American who didn't believe in traditional family values. Who knew Jane Austin could bring out such oddities in her readers?

It was Griggs who broke the silence. "In my defence, none of this would have happened if it weren't for that damned cat. He's always brought out the worst in me. With all the yowling and swiping, it's enough to drive a man to drink."

As Nan examined the wound, Griggs reeled off a list. "We need unpasteurized honey, black pepper, warm salted water, clean rags, and two baby aspirins."

I knew Nan would be too exasperated to speak, so I spoke for her. "For what?"

"So I don't get proud flesh. That's what my father would do whenever one of his horses got injured. And what was good enough for his best mounts, is good enough for me."

While Nan was scrounging up the supplies, and using more than her fair share of foul language, Griggs pulled a book out of her handbag. "We don't have long, so let's get down to business." Her voice was barely above a whisper. "I got this from the library, just like you instructed."

"That book on Morse code?" I asked.

"Of course. But I can't figure out why you wanted it."

"Archibald's been blinking at me."

"I see. That makes sense. Were some of her blinks quick like dots and others long like dashes?"

I closed my eyes and thought. "Kind of both," I said.

"That's good," Griggs said, before turning and yelling at Nan that she didn't want just any old rags. She wanted Nan to rip up an old flannel sheet to wrap the wound. She said it helped with blood flow. "Got to keep the old gal busy. She'll never understand modern communication." Griggs flipped the book open. "Now, Archibald doesn't strike me as the most ambitious person, so I'm assuming the message was simple— one of two things." She paused and listened for Nan. Nan was somewhere upstairs, probably going through her linen cupboard. "Was it .. .----. -- / ... --- .-. .-. -.--? Or more like .. / .... .- - . / -.-- --- ..- .-. / --. ..- - ... / --. . - / .-.. --- ... -?"

I shrugged.

"Think about it, it's important. One means *I'm sorry*, the other means *I hate your guts, get lost*."

I was leaning towards *I'm sorry*, but didn't get a chance to say so, because that's when Nan came back, arms laden with all of Griggs' demands.

"The next thing you'll want is for me to cauterize the wound," Nan said, arranging her supplies on the coffee table.

Griggs snorted as she slid the book back into her handbag. "You must think I'm a barbarian. What self-respecting book club would sanction the aroma of scorched flesh? Maybe for a war book, or something overly religious, but Jane Austen? She'd be rolling in her grave. Even the PIS ladies would steer clear of that one. Sometimes, Molly, you go too far."

"I go too far? Who in their right mind would believe that?"

"I would," Griggs said, slipping off her knee-highs.

Taking a scoop of honey, Nan plopped it into my palm as we prepared to slather the back of Griggs' leg. "The least you can do is hold still."

"I am," Griggs snapped. "I can't help it if my leg has a mind of its own."

"Please give me strength," Nan mumbled, as she held up Griggs' leg for me to slather the back of it. It was more disappointing than nauseating. I thought there would have been a far bigger gash with all the fuss Griggs made. Even so, by the time it was all wrapped and bound, Nan's fire had pretty much fizzled out, and it wasn't hard to talk her into giving our book club one last chance. Even Walter Douglas seemed to think it was a good idea, although he never said so.

While Griggs and me settled into our former spots, Nan

hushed Walter. It was something to watch. Griggs munched contently on the popcorn I had harvested from her hair, as Nan's melodic voice calmed the dark places of Walter's mind. Griggs said it was better than live television; even *The Edge of Night* couldn't pull such emotion out of its characters. When Walter's face had the look of partially melted butter, Nan sighed deeply and found her page.

"*A gentleman carrying a gun…*"

Griggs rubbed her hands together. "I like him already."

Nan paused, sucking in her nostrils. It was all that was needed. "*With two pointers playing round him, was passing up the hill and within a few yards of Marianne, when her accident happened…..*"

By the time our group called it a night, almost everything was forgiven. Walter promised to keep Tiberius locked up on book club nights. But in case the cat was out on the prowl and nowhere to be found, Nan vowed she'd bar the doors and windows.

Griggs was still adamant that someone owed her a new pair of hose. And Nan was adamant that it had been an act of God, something no one could have predicted or controlled. Griggs was not convinced, but said for the sake of the book club she'd let it go this time. But if that cat ever attacked her again there would be hell to pay.

"Duly noted," Nan said.

As Nan and me cleaned up after book club, she began to giggle. "As long as I live," she said, "I'll never forget the look on Dorigen's face. I thought she was so engrossed with Marianne that she'd lost her senses."

I nodded, but deep down inside I was thinking. Griggs hadn't lost anything. She had the sense to get Nan out of the room when she wanted. But I didn't want to tell Nan that. Being outfoxed was one thing; knowing about it was another.

13

After our invigorating book club meeting, the school day was a dismal affair. The days were growing colder, so no more trouncing around with my coat unbuttoned. And even worse, Miss Dobbs droned, Eugenia glowered, and Archibald was looking so much like the sickly Helen that I was starting to think it was a self-fulfilling prophesy. The only bright spot was teaching Timmy Crybaby-Head to Frankenstein-walk. "Timmy," I said, "if you don't adjust your bolty neck properly, no one is going to take you seriously."

He looked from me to Archibald. "You don't think she'll mind?"

"I doubt it." I didn't tell Timmy that I'd stopped asking Archibald anything. Not to teeter-totter, harpoon Nan, and definitely not to Frankenstein-walk with me through the freshly fallen leaves. But now that he mentioned it, I wondered if she missed galumphing in one another's shadows as much as I did. With every trudge Timmy and me took away from her, my heart ripped, but Archibald didn't seem to notice. She and Eugenia had spent the entire recess trading the same sweater. "Oh, that looks so much better on you," Eugenia said.

"No, I think it looks better on you." Archibald blushed.

Eugenia shrugged her shoulders as if she didn't have it in her to argue. "You're probably right."

Timmy straightened his neck before interjecting. "I think it would look better on me."

I turned and looked him up and down. He had a point, considering his colouring. I decided to employ another one of the pearls of wisdom Griggs had gleaned from Dale Carnegie: *give honest and sincere appreciation.* "I've always seen you as a sweater set man."

Timmy's face brightened. "That's what my mom thinks."

Griggs was right. After our hallway encounter and recess instruction, Timmy's floodgates of affection seemed to have opened from a drip to a trickle. When we returned to class, he didn't make me chase him around the room when we were supposed to be planning our Spooktacular project. Instead he feigned exhaustion after only two passes. I could have hugged him. And by the time the next recess rolled around, he offered me first dibs on his dead fly collection. "I'd rather not," I said. "Nan would have a bird. She's picky when it comes to playing with insect carcasses."

"Have it your way," he said, as he sprawled out in the dirt, lining up flies according to which retained most of their body parts. I watched him, mesmerized. Who knew Crybaby-Head could have an interesting side? One that didn't include leaky bladders and their unintended consequences. It made me full-body sigh.

Timmy stiffened, and without looking up he said, "You're falling in love with me, aren't you?"

I almost swallowed my tongue. "No!"

"Just wondering. That's the noise my mom makes whenever my dad mentions the mechanic."

"Oh," I said. "Hence you and your dad letting the air out of her tires so she can't take the car in for a tune up?"

He moved the flies into a different formation before nodding.

It felt good to have a school arm-length companion. I was reluctant to use the word *friend*. That might imply we liked one another. Which we definitely didn't. We tolerated each other. It was the same foundation that Griggs' and Nan's friendship was based on. One of mutual indifference. After all these years of getting on each other's nerves, they were almost inseparable.

It wasn't as if we were going to play on my sailboat bed as Captain Ahab and Queequeg, but it was a start.

My musings dissolved when I heard the words, *Helen, oh Helen*. I narrowed my eyes and turned toward the source. Eugenia Whitford, the blight of the Happy Valley School for Reluctant Children, was flaunting my *Jane Eyre* game in my face.

"I'm over here, Helen." Eugenia waved from the top of the monkey bars. Archibald slogged in that direction, giving the merry-go-round a wide berth. Probably because I'd told her witches lived beneath the underbelly of that wicked disk, quietly waiting for wayward children to wander too close.

"Do not," she'd said, knowing full well that I was the resident expert on the location and daily habits of local witches.

"Do too."

She'd shaken her head, indifferent to my warning.

"Have you ever heard of Emerson Elfelt?" I raised a cautious eyebrow.

"No."

"Neither have I," I said. "And there is only one reason he's been banned to the annals of oblivion: merry-go-rounds."

By the way Archibald was eyeing that wondrous contraption, I knew I was still making a difference in her life.

Anyways, Archibald climbed the bars to reach Eugenia's side. It was something I'd have never encouraged her to do. Even a fool could see Helen's skin was paper thin and could tear on the paint-chipped bars. I wanted to shout, *Where are her gloves?* But how was that neophyte supposed to know? Her nan didn't read her *Jane Eyre* while snuggled under a pile of quilts. She probably didn't even have a nan. Back when I was Jane, I was thoughtful. I didn't even consider marrying Mr. Rochester until his wife had burned to death.

But not anymore. Eugenia Whitford had replaced me, and obviously Archibald had divulged all the secrets of my story-book friends into her waxy ears. Now Jane was no longer that sweet girl, but was all covered with pustules and warts. Her name soured in my mouth.

"Helen," the new Jane said, syrupy sweet. "Do you think Mr. Rochester will want to play with us today?"

"He did yesterday," Helen replied, precariously balancing on her thin iron perch.

Some kids had stopped playing and started peering up at the monkey bars. They were making a spectacle of themselves.

"Oh no, not that Mr. Rochester. A real one." Warty Jane flung her arms wide. "Mr. Grenway Rochester."

That was a bridge too far. Grenway was Archibald's older brother. He was two fathers before Archibald's, and he had dimples. Whenever he smiled, I longed to poke my fingers in those divots. It made me trill inside. The thought of Eugenia doing the poking made me want to rip out her hair.

"Jane, I've already told you he won't answer to Rochester, Celia already tried. Besides, he never plays with girls."

Eugenia wrinkled her nose. "Well, I'm not Celia, am I?"

Archibald shrugged, and all the kids laughed.

I could feel my cheeks burning. I had no choice; I breathed

in Boudicca. "Crybaby-Head," I said, tapping Timmy on the shoulder. He ignored me. I jabbed him between his shoulder blades, and that got his attention. "Want to throw dead flies at Eugenia?"

Timmy turned, but it was Sir Percy Blakeney that smiled back at me.

14

Timmy was by my side before the last bell stopped its clanging. "Boudicca," he whispered, "what's our next adventure?"

I never knew throwing dead flies could capture a boy's heart so completely. Eugenia didn't know what hit her. Partly because the flies were so light and, having only dead wings to propel them, fell helplessly at our feet, coming nowhere near her dismal presence. It was anticlimactic, but as Griggs would say, it was the thought that counts. Before I had a chance to divulge what wonderful mayhem we could wade into next, Eugenia spotted us.

"They're staring at us."

"Who?" Archibald asked, without turning around.

"You know. The comic strip freak and its sidekick. Or Thing 1 and Thing 2. Take your pick."

My back stiffened, and I was pretty sure Timmy was about to dribble. "Steady on, Sir Percy," I muttered. "Steady on."

"Did Thing 1 say something?"

Archibald shrugged. I waited for her to turn and blink, but nada.

"No matter." Eugenia grabbed Archibald's hand and dragged her down the hall. "Who has time for a comic strip freak?"

I wanted to yell, *You, obviously! Otherwise why would you be hanging around with Archibald? She's as much of a comic strip freak as I am.* But somehow the words stuck in my throat. Blurting out that Archibald's fathers died as if it were a national pastime would only make me as obnoxious as Eugenia. Besides, *The Deadman's Wife* only ran when my comic strip was on hiatus. No use getting into which strip carried the most gravitas. It would be beneath my dignity.

I had to admit, though, it was hard to compete with husbands who died from such unusual deaths. It boggled the mind. The first got hit by a train while crossing a trestle. The second was much less creative. He froze. The third, Archibald's dad, got struck by lightning. The fourth died of rabies. The fifth got swarmed by bees. And last but not least, the sixth drowned. It was a cornucopia of tragedy.

"I heard her saying the poem," Crybaby-Head said, nodding at Eugenia and pulling me out of my musings.

"What poem?"

"You know. The one about Archibald's dads. She was singing it to the Grade Threes in the girl's bathroom. They said she was cute."

Although it irked me that Eugenia would sing Oswald Elliot's little ditty to entertain some empty-headed nincompoops, that's not the first thing that caught my attention. "What were you doing in the girl's bathroom?"

"That's my happy place."

I patted him on the arm. A pink-tiled bathroom—that made sense.

"She's a pretty good singer," Timmy went on. "Even though I hated what she was singing."

No one I cared about liked that poem. Nan wouldn't even discuss it, and Old Lady Griggs only memorized it so she could mock Oswald for his lack of literary prowess. My gaze caught Timmy's, and I knew those dastardly words were ear-worming their way into his mind as surely as they were into mine.

> Grenway Tibbs was crossing the tracks, was hit
>   by a train, now he's not coming back.
> Bose Malloy as strong as an ox, got stuck in a
>   snowdrift and came home in a box.
> Archibald Quigley, so sprite and so spry, rode his
>   bike through a meadow, how fast he did fry.
> Button Malloy, brother to Bose, was bit by a dog
>   and went mad to his toes.
> Earl McGinty, so brave and so true, stepped on a
>   hive, and now he's quite blue.
> Sly Willoughby, the best of the bunch, used his
>   car for a boat, don't expect him for lunch.

At the thought of it, I could feel the heat rise in my cheeks. For all my pontificating, I was no better than Eugenia Whitford. Although I hadn't sung about Archibald's melancholy experience for all and sundry, I'd certainly thought about it. Whenever she played Jane Eyre with her new best friend, or refused to take my plasticine telephone call, it was the first thing that tried to slip into my thoughts. But when Timmy told me about Eugenia singing it in the girls' bathroom, I knew even I couldn't sink that low. That mean poem was the only thing that tied me to Archibald now. It made me want to shield her from one more misery. The misery of Eugenia Whitford.

"Sir Percy," I said, "we don't have a moment to waste. It's time to rescue Marguerite St. Just."

15

It took me about two seconds to convince Timmy Crybaby-Head to tail Eugenia and Archibald. At the mention of his nom de plume, he was altered like a dog after a bone. His thin lips tightened until they were only a slash of determination. He was off on Eugenia's trail before I'd cleared my throat and stepped into my Boudicca persona. It galled me a little, since Crybaby-Head didn't even have story-book friends. He didn't spend his days slipping from Queequeg to Anna Karenina without running a comb through his hair. Nan thought it was remarkable, although she never said so out loud.

As I watched the transformation of Crybaby-Head, I was dumbstruck. With Archibald there were always questions like, *Does this one have warts?* Or, *Do their eyes get eaten by cats?* She was so predictable. But with Timmy there was nothing. He slid into Sir Percy as if it was his second skin. As if there were no reason for me at all. I didn't get to tell him about Sir Percy's favourite foods, or how he favoured natural to synthetic fabrics. It made me want to punch him in the head.

"Percy?" I called.

Timmy halted mid-step, and without turning around he said, "That's *Sir* Percy to you."

Now for sure I was going to punch him. He neglected to understand that I was *lending* him a storybook friend, not giving him one. He couldn't haphazardly rummage through the hours of reading I'd invested, cherry-picking what suited him best. I felt as indignant as Miss Libby, Happy Valley's town librarian, whenever Old Lady Griggs darkened the library door. I wanted to scream, *I'm the one who sets the rules. I'm the one who's in charge.* But he didn't seem to care. I trotted to catch up to him. "Crybaby-Head."

His hands balled into fists, but he didn't break his stride.

"Sir Percy," I begrudgingly corrected myself. His shoulders relaxed. "Don't you think we should make a plan?"

A visible shudder ran through him. "A plan? We're saving Lady Blakeney, that's the plan." He continued down the hall and out the door without turning around to see if I was following.

I rolled my eyes, and from somewhere deep inside I knew I was going to miss the old Crybaby-Head. How could I have taken him for granted? With a deep breath I inhaled Boudicca, letting her fierceness overflow and drip from my fingertips. I could almost feel the dirt between my toes, the sinew of partially cooked meat wedged between my teeth. Now I was ready. My gaze fixed on the school door. It was time to catch up to Sir Percy.

Stepping out into the afternoon light, I spied the good sir picking his way across the playground. To my astonishment, he wasn't trudging as he usually did, avoiding the sandbox, shunning the teeter-totter. No, he almost traipsed through the space. No longer did he care if the sand flies stuck to his pee-soaked legs, or that the unsteady teeter-totter might be deliberately used by the older boys to catapult him through the air if he stepped too close. As Boudicca, I grunted my approval; as Celia, I thought him foolhardy.

Sir Percy, I almost said, *you really must rein yourself in.* But before the words flew out of my mouth, I remembered who I was. Boudicca. She would never ask, she would demand. "Percy," I barked. "Heel!"

But my words must have got caught on the gentle autumn breeze. He didn't even break his stride. This would not do. "Crybaby-Head," I thundered, reverting back to his Christian name. "I didn't lend you one of my storybook friends so you could ignore my edicts!" As if he'd know what that word meant. "I lent him to you so you could be my lesser-known sidekick. The one who stands in the background and waits for my instructions."

This fell on deaf ears. Crybaby-Head was impervious. I might as well have been talking to Griggs. I increased my stride and thought about the best way to pummel him without drawing blood. Then it occurred to me that this might be counterproductive. If I wanted someone to help me save Archibald, Crybaby-Head fit the bill to a tee. And as Sir Percy he seemed to think of himself as invincible, which made him perfect cannon fodder.

While Sir Percy and me were dodging behind boulders and ducking into the rough, Jane and Helen were skipping and arm swinging. To be more precise, Jane was doing all the prancing, and Helen's anemia seemed to be acting up. As Jane skipped, the toes of Helen's shoes skimmed the path, leaving a trail of dust in her wake. I couldn't decide if she was doing so out of lethargy, or if she was intuitively aware of my presence and leaving me a bread crumb trail of scuff marks. The path was so well worn that, if I hadn't known where it was, I could have found her house in the dark. Still, I warmed at the thought.

As Sir Percy and me continued our subterfuge, I marveled at

his dexterity. Not only was he apt at serpentine walking, camouflage seemed to be his forte as well. His plaid pants and checkered shirt blended perfectly with the fall foliage. But all our antics were for naught. Not once did Eugenia glance in our direction. Not once did she pull Archibald to a halt and shout, *Stop following us.* It was as if we weren't worth the effort.

Even from our untenable position—between a bunch of half-dead nettles and thorns from a rose bush tearing holes in my clothes—I could catch whispers of the most unrealistic dialogue imaginable. Charlotte Brontë would have been horrified.

"Helen," Eugenia simpered, "when we get to your house let's have tea. I'll be mother."

"Jane, you're always mother," Archibald pouted.

"That's because I'm best at it, silly. You'd probably spill and mess the whole thing up. That would be a disaster." She tapped Archibald on the tip of her nose. "And what's a best friend for, if not to protect you from disaster? Besides, my Aunt Enid is a member of The Ladies of the Perpetual Indigence Society, and they have high tea at every meeting. It's in the Whitford blood." She paused and looked scornfully at Archibald. "Do you even know what high tea is?"

Archibald shook her head.

"I didn't think so. That's why I need to pour."

I couldn't take it anymore. I sprung from my hiding spot. "Enough is enough," I said, letting my Boudicca voice rise above my adversary's. "She's not a spiller, and if you loved her the way I do, you'd know that."

Sir Percy stood as abruptly as I had, bravely ignoring the rosebush thorns that raked his skin. "Ditto," he echoed.

Eugenia chuckled, dismissing us with a wave of her hand. "Ignore them Archibald," she said. "It's your mother you should be concerned about. Remember what I told you?"

For a second I thought Archibald was going to pull her hand away from Eugenia's, adjust her bolty neck, and let loose her draggy leg. But she didn't. And when Eugenia started to skip away, Archibald shuffled along beside her, as if I'd said nothing at all.

I wanted to shout, *She sings about you in the bathroom, you know? Sings to the Grade Threes about how all your dads died.* But I knew Eugenia would only turn it back on me. Say that it was me doing the singing and how she'd begged me to stop.

For the rest of the way to Archibald's house, I couldn't listen to Eugenia's prattle. Her mean words had chased the Boudicca in me away, I was nothing now but plain old Celia. It was all I could do not to pummel her to the ground, but I wasn't sure if Sir Percy was up to being my second. We were nothing more than faceless proletariats following in their wake. I reached out and grabbed Sir Percy's hand, finding comfort where I could, and hating Eugenia for forcing me to do so.

Only when Fanny Figgler, Archibald's neighbour and one of the banes of my existence, called to me was I startled out of my stupor.

"What are you up too, Celia Canterberry?" She hurled herself towards us. "No good, I suspect." Before I could answer, her eyes darted toward Sir Blakeney. "And who's your funny little friend?"

From the corner of my eye I spied Sir Blakeney. He hadn't even registered the insult. I stuck up for him anyway. "I won't dignify that with a response," I said.

"Of course not. You're much too la-di-da for that. Thinking you're so fancy because your grandmother owns a dictionary."

I wanted to tell her not to lose heart, that even a dolt like her could own a book with words in it, but I didn't get a chance. Fanny Figgler had fixed her attention back on Sir Blakeney. She was out for blood.

"He's not a member of the European Cheese Tasters, because I'd remember a face like that. I'm an encyclopedia when it comes to faces."

She stepped forward before immediately drawing back. "Timmy Leach." Her voice soured. "Caroline Dobbs said you could smell that one coming."

"Caroline Dobbs said," I mimicked. "But he's not Timmy Leach today. He's not even Timmy Crybaby-Head." It was my only defence. Fanny Figgler would never understand my storybook friends and how I lent them out like library books.

"Who is he then?"

I turned to Timmy. He stood frozen in the middle of the street that ran between Figgler's house and Archibald's. His finger-leaves fluttered in the breeze. He'd never looked more like a non-speaking tree. My heart filled with pride. "Well," I began, "it's hard to tell at this very moment. It's like he's perplexed. On a precipice, so to speak. Should he be a deciduous sapling?" Timmy shifted, balancing on his tiptoes, hands curled in front of him like a prancing pony. "Or perhaps the dependable Homo sapien?"

Fanny Figgler snorted. "Once again Enid Whitford was right. She said you were just a twenty-five cent girl using five dollar words. I had to agree. Said just the other day, 'teaching an interior a few fancy words doesn't make her any less of an interior.'"

"No one has ever accused you of being a linguist, have they?"

"I should hope not."

It was hard to believe we were related. Fanny Figgler was the sister of my should-have-been paternal grandfather. And it was because of this unwanted family connection that I couldn't help but correct her diction. It was my duty to stretch her limited vocabulary. "But I think you meant *inferior*, not interior.

A common mistake for someone who has an aversion to proficiency."

Fanny looked momentarily confused. "Don't tell me what I think." She glared at me as her kaleidoscope muumuu fluttered. No doubt a fart had got caught in its expanse and was now fighting to get free. Timmy Crybaby-Head, or whoever he was at the moment, was forgotten.

16

Soon after that, Fanny Figgler disappeared into her house. Sadly though, not due to our conversational impasse. It was because her son, Skinny, had stepped out onto the veranda whining that he was starving and couldn't find the jam.

"It's where it always is. In the fridge," she bellowed, as she crossed her yard with remarkable speed. "And don't tell me you can't open the jar. It's not that hard. Counter clockwise to open, clockwise to close. Didn't they teach you anything at school? If you can't manage that, how in the world do you expect to woo Lacey?" Without even turning, she jabbed a pudgy finger at Archibald's house. "That one is ripe for the picking. I can smell it from here." The screen door slammed, and her voice began to fade away. "All the brawn of Charles Atlas and the brains of Gomer Pyle."

As soon as the door closed my eavesdropping was cut off, and just when it was getting to the very best part. In a way though, I almost felt sorry for Fanny. She had moved to Happy Valley in hopes of marrying her son off to Archibald's mom. It was no secret that the six-time widow had gained a small fortune from all the life insurance claims. A man could acquire a pocketful of wealth just by saying *I do*. But if her son couldn't even open a jar of jam, he probably wouldn't have a lot of luck turning Archibald's mom's head.

I turned back to Timmy, who seemed to have settled on the persona of Sir Percy Blakeney, his hands permanently curled like an old arthritic woman. No self-respecting tree would strike that pose, not even on the windiest of days. Even Eugenia was staring, her thin lips curled into a snarl. She snorted before tugging Archibald's arm. "Let's go have tea," she said, and the two of them stepped into Archibald's house. But before they disappeared, I swear Archibald blinked in my direction.

"Did you see that?" I loud-whispered, but there was no one there to loud-whisper back. Sir Percy, nose in the air, was high-knee prancing his way across the street. He probably hadn't even noticed Archibald sending me a secret message. "Sir Percy," I snapped.

Not even a grunt.

"I've already warned you. Do you want to be a nonspeaking tree again? Remember how much fun that was?"

That got his attention. Sir Percy turned, drilling me with steely eyes. It was as if he saw right through me, but now that he was a knight of the queen's realm he could ignore me with impunity, and there was nothing I could do about it. Not even Eugenia Whitford could penetrate me like that. I wanted to kick him. How could Timmy Crybaby-Head so easily become the fussbudget Sir Percy, and me, who'd been morphing into my storybook friends for as long as I could remember, couldn't seem to hold on to Boudicca? Dirt-under-her-nails Boudicca, who was probably off somewhere plundering some warring Roman! Boudicca, who could have easily been my namesake, if Nan had had the foresight to name me after her.

I stomped my foot. It didn't help.

Boudicca once again slipped out of my grasp. I'd have to settle for Celia. Plain old Celia.

Sir Percy rolled his Crybaby-Head eyes, and flipped his arthritic hand as if I were little more than one of his dead flies. I had no choice but to be his sidekick; his Archibald. I bit my lip. I was pretty sure Archibald didn't even want to be anyone's Archibald anymore.

Begrudgingly, I slinked after him, until the two of us were directly under Mrs. Willoughby's kitchen window. We stood on our tip toes and peered inside. My eyes nearly popped out of my head. There, at the Willoughby's kitchen table, Eugenia and Archibald were having tea, and Eugenia was pouring. She looked like the cat that swallowed the canary. Her free hand waved through the air, probably talking about her Chatty Cathy doll. That wasn't so bad. I'd been expecting it, preparing for it ever since I heard Eugenia mention it while we were stalking her.

The galling part was that Archibald's older brother, Grenway, had joined them! He made the worst Mr. Rochester imaginable. Instead of smoking a pipe and feigning indifference, he drank from his little china cup as if it were an everyday occurrence. And as far as I knew, it was. I was so disappointed in him. If he truly had an ounce of Rochester in him, he'd hogtie Eugenia and lock her in the attic with his wife—not stare at her as if she were a prized zoo exhibit. I'd have to rethink putting my fingers in his dimple divots.

But what was worse, Sir Percy had puckered up and was kissing the fly-speckled pane. I jabbed him in the ribs, but his suction-cupped lips held firm. "Sir Percy, even I think that's weird. Marguerite St. Just will be horrified, and who will marry you then?"

He unsuctioned, devastation stamped on his visage.

"We should check out the other windows. You never know

what else might lurk behind this thin veneer they call happiness."

Sir Percy nodded. Thank God he was a man of few words. We weaved our way to the back of the house. Leafless quaking aspens, chokecherry, and Saskatoon bushes tried to bar our way. "Watch your step, Sir Percy," I said, as I pulled back branches and stepped over rotting logs. Following my lead, Sir Percy matched me step for step, never once fussing over the arduous terrain. I almost regretted dubbing him Crybaby-Head. "Here," I said, pointing up to the window that looked into the extraordinary library—the library I wasn't supposed to know about; the room that Archibald had made me promise to keep secret, saying her mother hated having her life splashed all over that rag of a newspaper, and she wasn't going to give Oswald Elliot any ideas. I wasn't supposed to tell anyone, not even Nan —and especially not Griggs—and I had kept my word. Which surprised me as much as the next guy. That is until today, when Archibald's future husband and me gazed up at the spotless panes. But no matter how much we stretched and reached, we couldn't see over the window ledge.

"Sir Percy, do you mind?" I said, motioning him to get down on all fours. He looked indignant, as if such an act were beneath him. "For Marguerite's sake." I stifled a sob.

Before I had a chance to scrape the mud off the bottom of my shoes, Sir Percy was down on all fours, bracing himself for my weight. I curtsied before stepping up. Cupping my hands around the sides of my face I peered through the pane. Within an instant I was back, side by side with Archibald in the beloved room. Only this time it was my memory of Archibald that accompanied me. She had let me step through the majestic library doors after I'd touched their heavy knockers, brass hands clasping apples. She'd led me through stacks of unshelved books and dusty boxes, and at the end of our endless weaving, gestured towards the glorious clock from Prague. The same clock I spied now as I remembered Archibald's spiel.

"There are four figures flanking the clock," I heard her distant voice say. "Vanity is represented by the figure in the short green robe admiring himself in the mirror. Next is the Miser. He is represented by the greedy man holding a bag of gold. Lust, the love of earthly pleasures, holds the lute. And last but not least, Death is represented by the skeleton who on the hour rings his bell, warning that he could come at any time. As he rings, Lust, Vanity, and the Miser shake their heads, indicating they are not ready to go."

I warmed at the memory. "Miss me?" I whispered to the clock. And as if answering, the skeleton rang the bell. I shook my head right along with the Miser, Lust, and Greed. It was good to be back.

That's when Sir Percy began to fuss. "My turn," he said, with such authority I knew he wouldn't be dissuaded.

"All right," I said, climbing down and readying myself to take his place. It was the last thing I wanted to do. Regardless of the falling out I'd had with Archibald, there was something in me that bristled at the thought of betraying her. "But only a quick look," I said. "Mrs. Willoughby is dusting." Although, truth be told, Archibald's mother was nowhere in sight.

"I've seen dusting before," he said, a little cavalierly. "My mother does it at least once a week."

"Have it your way," I said, as he set his first foot on my back. "But she dusts in the nude. Saves on laundry."

17

After Sir Percy finished throwing up, he said he didn't feel that a gentleman like himself should be peering through windows. I nodded in agreement before we bushwhacked our way back to the front of Archibald's house. When we rounded the corner, Mrs. Willoughby was hanging sheets, her head and rubber boots being the only things visible to us. Sir Percy stopped dead in his tracks. I stepped aside, in case he hadn't totally emptied his stomach.

"Do you think she's dressed?" he asked.

I shrugged. "Who knows with widows? They're an unpredictable lot."

Without another word we each touched the side of our nose, slipped back into the bush, and went our separate ways.

Inside, my heart was bursting; outside, my feet were skipping. Seeing that death-judgment clock had untwisted my lungs and lifted my spirits. In celebration, I was off to see Samwise Gamgee in Farmer Hempel's field. The thought of Samwise Gamgee, Farmer Hempel's horse, sniffing me after I'd dodged his wild roan cow was rather appealing. Eugenia would hate that, and anything Eugenia hated was well worth doing.

When I caught sight of the yard, Farmer Hempel was up to his knees in fallen leaves. He was muttering to himself. I'd seen his look before. Nan often struck that pose when Griggs slipped into the nonsensical. But as soon as we clapped eyes on each other, he brightened.

"Celia," he beamed. When I didn't beam back, his smile faltered. "Still on the outs with Archibald?"

I nodded.

"Well, don't worry my dear. These things have a way of working themselves out."

I hoped so. The thought of scaring off Eugenia and resuming my Frankenstein-walking with Archibald made my heart flutter.

"Perhaps I can cheer you up." He scratched his chin. "I've got some good news."

"Good news?" It was an odd thing for a farmer to say.

"Yes. Sold Wild Roan this morning."

That *was* good news! I hated that cow. She thought she was so fancy with her French-sounding name. Roan! Even if you rolled the r, how fancy could she be? She pooped in a field. Besides, excluding the Whitfords, Miss Dobbs, and Fanny Figgler—my other human nemesis—she was the bane of my existence. That cow made out as if we were as close as two peas in a pod, scratching the ground and lowering her head in what I can only describe as a cow curtsy, before trying to impale me with her crumpled horns.

Farmer Hempel hooked his thumbs in his suspender straps. "To be honest, I didn't want to sell her. We'd made our peace, and as long as I stayed out of her way, she stayed out of mine." His head jerked towards his house. "But it wasn't the same with the Mrs. That old gal had a habit of busting through the fence. Wild Roan, that is. And like clockwork, it always seemed to happen at the same time my wife was fussing about the yard, pulling a weed here, planting a daisy there. While she was fussing about, Wild Roan was zoning in, and then the race was on. It didn't matter what I tried—whether adding an extra line of barbed wire or fixing her with a cow poke—that cow was bound and determined to get my wife. She had it in for her, but this last time was the last straw.

"We were raking leaves," he continued, shading his eyes with his hand. "And I tell you what, we couldn't have asked for a nicer day. It was pretty much the same as it is now—a warm sun, a light breeze. I was whistling, and my Mrs. was humming along, harmonizing the way happily married couples do. But that's when it all went to hell in a handbasket. I don't know who heard the bellow first, but the Mrs. was the first to scream. Her eyes were saucers as she turned and raced for the house, hell-bent for leather. To be honest, my Mrs. has never been much of a runner, and age hasn't done her any favours. As she threw herself forward, Wild Roan honed in. I did the only thing I could. I grabbed hold of that old cow's horns, dug in my heels, and twisted her to the ground, like the steer wrestlers in the rodeo. Except age hasn't done me any favours either. My twist was more of a tug, and besides slowing her a little and leaving a trail of dust, I was just a minor inconvenience. Still, it was enough to let my Mrs. escape."

"I bet she was thankful."

"Not really. Even though she was screaming like a banshee, somehow she heard me chuckle. I couldn't help myself. The whole situation struck me funny. That woman can't hear me call when I'm out of toilet paper, but she can make out a tiny chortle in all that ruckus? It's enough to make a preacher swear." He looked back at the house. "Didn't speak to me for over a week, and when she did, it was to demand I sell Wild Roan. Said it was that cow or her. I said I'd think about it, and the next morning told her I'd made my decision. The cow would go. And you know what irks me most?"

I shook my head.

"She got what she wanted, and she's still not speaking to me. Between you and me, Celia, there is no pleasing some women."

"Is that the good news?"

Farmer Hempel looked stunned for a moment. "No, no. The good news is you can traipse through my pasture anytime you like now. There's no bovine out to kill you."

I looked at Farmer Hempel doubtfully. My previous experiences didn't bear that out. The first time that cow attacked, during a lightning storm, was almost the end of me. If it hadn't been for Oswald Elliot and his intrepid banana-seat bike, I probably wouldn't be standing here today. The second time Farmer Hempel snatched me from the hooves of death, his big hands whipped me over the fence before I could say Jack Robinson.

The cows that occupied the space now meandered around, not seeming to care that their protector had probably been sold for dog food. Ingrates.

"And I'm getting a puppy."

"So he can eat your cow?"

"No." Farmer Hempel frowned. "What an odd thing to say. The puppy's to appease the Mrs. She's wanted one for years, but I thought why get a dog? Every farm has a dog, and the last thing I want to be is a cliché."

Looking at his overalls, plaid shirt, and straw hat, I thought, *That ship has sailed.* Still, the thought of a puppy thrilled me, even though it wouldn't be mine. It could lick me and hump my leg, like Billy Billboson's dog does. Billy says there is no greater show of affection.

"Think I'll let the little woman name it," Farmer Hempel

continued. "Even let her bring it into the house." He raised his eyebrows, as if I should be impressed by his concessions. "But I digress. What I really wanted to talk to you about was Fade. The wife's horse."

"Samwise Gamgee," I corrected him.

"Samwise. I forgot. It's not every day that your animals get renamed by a little trespasser. Anyhow, now that Wild Roan has moved on, you can take that shortcut through the pasture. Spend time with Samwise after school."

That was the best news I'd heard in a long time. Spending time with Samwise without getting trampled was the thing of dreams. It would almost be as good as spending time with Archibald. I wanted to throw my arms around Farmer Hempel, and would have if he didn't have so many brown smudges on his overalls.

Forcing down one wire with his work boot and pulling another one up with his gloved hand, he made space for me and grinned." After you, me lady."

I hesitated. "Are you sure you sold the right cow?"

Farmer Hempel turned and faced the herd, examining each cow in turn. "Yup, pretty sure." He winked. "But we'll soon find out."

I grimaced as I slipped through the opening.

That's when I heard him chuckle. "On second thought…"

His words made me freeze in my tracks.

"The look on your face," he beamed. "Same one my wife had. How so much fuss can be made by one cow is beyond me." He chuckled again before joining me on the other side of the fence. "Let me introduce you to my herd."

We picked our way across the pasture—fresh cow-pies here, road apples there. "Some of the old girls might get curious, come a little close. If it makes you uncomfortable, wave your arms and shout like this." Farmer Hempel raised his arms above his head and bellowed at the bovines. They scuttled back. "You try."

I looked from Farmer Hempel to the cows.

"Go ahead. They don't bite."

That's when I roared, letting out everything I'd kept pent up inside. A great aunt that I didn't want. A best friend that didn't want me. And too many nemeses to name. My lips trembled as all my misery began rising up and reverberating out of my voice box. It felt good. Bertha-Mason-laughing-like-a-madwoman good.

Farmer Hempel took a step back, aghast. "You could give my wife a run for her money."

I smiled and he formally introduced me to Samwise Gamgee. (Sam and me had chatted over the fence before. I'd given him a carrot and he'd breathed on my cheek. We were practically betrothed.)

"Fade," Farmer Hempel said with great formality, "I secretly name you Samwise Gamgee." He flicked his head towards me. "Samwise, this is Celia Canterberry. Celia Canterberry, this is Samwise."

I did a curtsy, and Sam nudged me with his nose.

"He wants to know if you have something for him in your pocket."

I shook my head.

"That's okay. He'll get over it."

Farmer Hempel showed me how to halter Sam and lead him to the board fence next to the barn. "After you've lined him up, climb the boards and slip on his back."

I did, and I knew by the way Sam nickered he'd been waiting for me his whole life. Lying flat on my tummy, I wrapped my arms around his neck. "I love you Samwise," I whispered. "You don't have to be my sidekick. You just have to hate Eugenia."

He seemed amenable, and at the mention of Eugenia's name, he pinned his ears, the same as Mister Ed does before he kicks someone. I patted his neck. Samwise was another arrow in my quiver.

"Now take the lead," Farmer Hempel instructed. "He's good with one rein." After that he taught me how to get Sam to move by squeezing my legs. "A little pressure is all he needs, and once he moves, relax."

Sam and me meandered all around the pasture, and once Farmer Hempel was confident things were in hand, he disappeared into the house. Said his wife might not be speaking to him, but that didn't mean she didn't want him underfoot.

18

As I kissed Samwise goodbye, I reminded him that I was Frodo and he had promised Gandalf never to leave me. And that I was pretty sure Aragon and Legolas, who were posing as nearby cows, heard him, so there was no use trying to get out of it now. Samwise blinked his blue eyes and nudged me with his velvety nose. We were of the same mind.

All the way down Main Street my feet barely touched the ground. It was one of the happiest days of my life—if I didn't count trying to shoehorn Timmy Crybaby-Head in as a substitute best friend. I didn't know what else to call him; 'anomaly' seemed too harsh.

I was also thankful our informal book club was gaining steam. Monitoring the story while keeping an eye on whatever antics Griggs and Walter Douglas were up to made the rest of the week bearable. I crunched a pile of gutter leaves before skipping wildly. That is, until I caught sight of Eugenia Whitford and Archibald Quigley. They were hand in hand, arms swinging to beat the band. At least Eugenia was swinging. Archibald was holding her shoulder as if she were suffering from some kind of repetitive injury. The only thing I could figure was that they must have slipped out of Archibald's house when I was riding Samwise. Served me right for allowing boundless joy to infect me. I should have taken a page from Griggs' book. She said scowling only gave you wrinkles, but a smile could lead to a broken heart.

Ceasing my exuberance, I shadowed the pair, doing my best Hercule Poirot, slipping noiselessly after them. To my dismay, neither of them stopped to pay homage at my sidewalk star as they passed the bakery. In fact, I was pretty sure Eugenia spit on it.

"Sacre bleu," I muttered under my breath. I knew it troubled Hercule to express himself in such a despicable manner, but as Nan says, desperate times required desperate, or in my case, *despicable* measures. Even Hercule would understand that.

As the girls crossed the street my heart almost stopped. I realized where they were heading. The Happy Valley Druggist. The one place Nan insisted I stay clear of. Well, maybe not the one place, but the one she badgered me most about. I blew out my cheeks, whispered an apology to Nan, and followed.

The bell at the top of the drugstore door rang and the girls disappeared inside. The last time I entered the Happy Valley Druggist, it hadn't turned out so well. I knocked over the sunglasses display, breaking the gumball machine, and that led to me having to cut off one of the Whitford owl-children's pigtails a little too close to the scalp. Hence, I had to colour in the bald spot with a Jiffy marker. It would have made sense if you'd been there.

Mr. Whitford made a fortune on Jiffy markers after that. His child was a living testament to their durability. Mrs. Whitford wasn't of the same mind. She never forgave me—not that she'd endeared herself to me before—hence my being relegated to the sidewalk. The fishwife tried to ban me from Main Street altogether, but the mayor said it was good for the public to catch a glimpse of the notorious subject of Oswald Elliot's comic strip.

Slipping alongside the drugstore I pressed my face into the glass, just like I'd done when I was spying at the clock in Archibald's house. This time, though, I had to tilt my gaze just to scan in between the displays of Toni Home Permanents and cod liver oil. And sure as shooting, I glimpsed Eugenia and Archibald at the candy counter. Nan was waiting on them, and I could tell by the way she held her mouth she wasn't pleased. She looked more put out than when we were playing Moby Dick on my sailboat bed and Archibald tried to harpoon her with a sharpened willow stick. The memory brought a smile to my face. Those were good days. Mid-grin I was rudely interrupted.

"What ya doing?"

I froze, but my mind whirled trying to place the voice. I hated being caught unaware; it gave me less time to decide if I should bolt or chat. That's when I looked down and glimpsed a pair of fluffy orange bedroom slippers. It was a dead giveaway! Agnes Obermeyer. What had thrown me off was that Griggs did a better Agnes Obermeyer voice than Agnes did. Agnes had never appreciated Griggs' genius.

"Window shopping," I said, turning to face her. And let me tell you, she was a sight for sore eyes. The scarf around her neck was red with white polka dots, her blouse—purple checkers, and her pants—green and blue stripes. She finished the look with her fluffy, dirt-encrusted orange bedroom slippers.

Seemingly aware of my appraisal, she waved her hand in front of her ensemble. "They were having a sale at Murry's Haberdashery."

"I'd sell those clothes too, if they were mine."

Agnes sniffed. "Aren't you one to talk? I've seen your comic strip; you're no Audrey Hepburn."

She had a point. It was hard to be trendy with a *Dick and Jane* reader for a head.

She tapped the pane. "What caught your eye? The Toni home perm or the cod liver oil? I'm a little plugged up myself."

I shrugged and wiped off the smudge marks I'd made with my sleeve. Nan was always going on about rude people who touched the drugstore window, making smears for her to clean.

"I've always wanted a home perm myself," Agnes went on. "Thought I'd look like an older Shirley Temple. Her post-actress stage. You know, when she was down and out after the shine wore off." The cigarette embedded in her crusty lipstick bobbed with every word. "But whenever I ask my sister to give me one, she yells, 'It's the middle of the night. Stop calling.' Enid's never been the same since she married that Whitford character. That, and after I set her hair on fire. Such a little thing. It's not like hair doesn't grow back. All I can say is, that woman can hold a grudge."

Agnes and Enid Whitford may have been sisters, but they weren't peas in a pod. In fact, Nan said they didn't even grow in the same garden. Mrs. Whitford wouldn't publicly claim her sibling, but Agnes screeched it from the rafters.

"I wish I had a sister that would hang up on me," I said, looking back to where Eugenia and Archibald were filling their loot bags.

"No you don't. They're not worth the effort." Agnes licked her finger and drew a broken heart on Nan's polished pane. She looked down at me and winked. "Maybe it's just you and me, sis."

The thought sent a shiver down my spine. Although I enjoyed my encounters with Agnes Obermeyer, I couldn't imagine the two of us skipping through the playground at recess or standing in the teeter-totter line. Timmy Crybaby-

Head and his dead flies were looking more appealing by the minute.

The longer I stood in front of the storefront window with Agnes Obermeyer by my side, the more I became aware of my nan. She wouldn't approve. If she caught me spying on the Whitfords, she'd skin me alive. Even if I claimed that it was Archibald I was stalking, she'd be unmoved. She'd say, *How many times have I told you, Celia?*

I'd shrug.

You can't go around borrowing trouble, she'd say. *I won't always be around to bail you out.*

I cringed at the hypothetical conversation. Even hypothetical Nan was hard to argue with.

What I wouldn't have told Nan was that whenever I got up the nerve I liked to walk by the drugstore, because it was like walking on gravel in my bare feet. It toughened me up. A touch of Whitford was the best preparation for a penitentiary fence encounter. Only it could make my should-have-been pa seem less intimidating. Facing a Whitford was akin to facing an orc. Still, it was wise advice at the time, and I couldn't fault Nan for trying.

Agnes interrupted my musings. "Although this is the highlight of my day, we're tempting fate. My sister hates me loitering outside her store. Had me arrested for it last week."

"Did you get bread and water?" I asked, searching her arms for prison tattoos.

"No." Agnes rolled her eyes in disgust. "A waste of taxpayers' dollars, as far as I'm concerned. The mayor sprung me. Said I'd taken a long enough lunch break, and the phone was ringing off the hook. I didn't even get a proper pat down."

"That's too bad," I said.

"You're telling me." Agnes' voice hardened. We stood a bit

longer examining our reflections. "You know what?" Agnes said, face brightening.

I shook my head.

"This window reminds me of a gigantic television screen. The kind that Lawrence Welk would kill for."

"Perhaps," I said. "But I don't think Mr. Welk is the type to get his hands dirty."

"Looks can be deceiving; he's German, after all."

Agnes' cigarette stopped bobbing, and her neck lengthened as if she were posing for the top of a wedding cake. Her toes pointed, and the dirt on her encrusted fluffy slippers knocked together like tiny castanets. "I'll be Bobby, you be Cissy."

"The dancers from The Lawrence Welk Show?"

"Who else?"

I shrugged. I've been book people before. Captain Ahab, Jane Eyre, Huck Finn, and Anna Karenina, to name a few. But I'd never been a television person. It wasn't as appealing. With book people I got to decide all their little details, the ones not stated explicitly, but with television people, there was nothing left to the imagination. My conundrum didn't faze Agnes, God bless her. And when one of her hands unfurled towards me, I wasn't sure what to do.

"I don't have all day," she snapped. "Are we going to dance or are you going to stand around and stare at me? If my sister is going to have me arrested, it might as well be as someone famous. Besides," her voice was almost a whisper, "we can show your little friend how much fun you are. What she's missing."

I looked towards Archibald, who was still standing at the candy counter. With enough commotion she might look our way and think, *Wow, I always wanted to be a Lawrence Welk dancer.* I knew it was a Hail Mary, but not being Catholic, I didn't think God would mind.

Shrugging, I took Agnes' hand. Dance it was. We pranced a circle in front of the drugstore window, smiles pasted on our faces, as Agnes imitated Lawrence Welk's introduction. *"Listen to that audience, what a beautiful audience. Greetings, friends, and welcome. This evening we bring you a showstopper. A sure-fire hit. The amazing dancing duo, Bobby and Cissy."*

I did the sound of cheering while Agnes pulled me in for what she said was a foxtrot. To me, it was a lot of jumping and turning. All the while, the both of us sang the only Lawrence Welk song we knew by heart.

> "Goodnight, goodnight, until we meet again.
> Adios, Au Revoir, Auf Wiedersehn, 'til then.
> And though it's always sweet sorrow to part.
> You know you'll always remain in my heart.
> Goodnight, sleep tight, and pleasant dreams
>   to you.
> Here's a wish and a prayer that every dream
>   comes true.
> And now, 'til we meet again, Adios, Au Revoir,
>   Auf Wiedersehn."

By the time the verse was done, Agnes was bent over, her hands on her knees. "You're not very light on your feet," she wheezed, her faithful cigarette clinging to its spot.

"I didn't know I had to be," I said, taken aback. The way she'd been swinging me around, I thought she was going to pull my arms out of their sockets. With the thought of having no arms, having an almost-friend smelling of pee no longer mattered. Neither did my should-have-beens or Miss Dobbs and her extra-long yardstick. Nothing was important if I had no arms.

Agnes was so caught up with being Bobby and Cissy, she

didn't realize we'd attracted a crowd. And Oswald Elliot, who should have been sketching to beat the band, was standing there, a little dazed. Without Griggs to guide him, the man was lost. Even without the cartoon rendering though, Nan would be furious if she caught me making a spectacle outside her place of work. I tried to slip away, but Agnes grabbed my elbow. "Where do you think you're going?

"Got to get ready for book club." I rubbed my shoulders.

"That can wait," Agnes said, taking a bow. "We're on a roll, and it's going to make Enid lose her mind." She turned to me. "Why are your eyes all red?"

"Bubbles," I lied. Anyone who even casually watched Mr. Welk knew he had a bubble fetish. Griggs had said it caused her to question his motives more than once. "Do you know how slick soap bubbles can make a dance floor? It's like watching a train wreck. That man doesn't like women." Then she'd turn up the volume on her television so she didn't miss what he was going to say next.

"A little imaginary soap never hurt anyone." Agnes grabbed my hand and was about to take another turn on the sidewalk, when her sister came bursting out the door. There was a collective gasp and most of the crowd stepped forward, committing to memory the minutest of details—just in case any of their future grandchildren asked, *Where were you when?*

Mrs. Whitford grabbed Agnes by her purple checkered blouse. "If I've told you once, I've told you a thousand times, no loitering!"

Prying Enid's fingers off one at a time, Agnes smirked. "Wasn't loitering." She pointed down at me. "We were Lawrence Welk dancing."

That was the straw that broke the camel's back. If Mrs. Whitford was furious before, now she was volcanic. "You," she sputtered, turning her rage on me. Her face was so taut that her glued-on eyelashes popped free at the edges. "I've told Molly to keep you clear of here. I've told her you're not welcome. Never will be. But no. She can't even accomplish that one simple thing."

I blinked. Why she was still upset was beyond me. Her little owl girl's hair had grown. I'd seen it myself. She looked as empty-headed as ever, though—the look of an owlet deliberately dropped from the nest. Mrs. Whitford raised her hand, and I was afraid she'd wallop me, when her husband stepped into the frame.

"What do we have here?" he asked, taking hold of his wife's sleeve.

No one answered.

"A bit of a vaudeville act?" he went on.

"Not vaudeville." Agnes' face reddened. "There are no pasties or fan dances here. What do you take us for? This is, if you'd been paying attention, our tribute to the great Lawrence Welk."

"A German who doesn't want to kill people," I added.

Mr. Whitford grunted his approval. "That's a selling point." He raised his gaze to the crowd. "Since you're all here, why not step inside and have my lovely wife serve you a fresh cup of complimentary coffee?"

His lovely wife blanched. "I'll do no such thing."

"Oh, isn't she sweet," he said, tightening his grip with one hand and smacking her on the bottom with the other.

Mrs. Whitford wrenched her arm free and stomped back into the drugstore.

"We'll see how many are served before the dishes start flying," Mr. Whitford chuckled, before bending down and whispering into my ear. "I'm going to give your nan a raise, with all this extra business you bring in."

There was a mumble as the crowd shifted. One by one they

followed Mr. Whitford back into his store, like a row of obedient ducklings.

I frowned, reached up, and took Agnes Obermeyer's hand. "I don't think Archibald noticed," I said.

"There's still hope." She tweaked my nose. "Especially if we get arrested."

19

After school I played on my sailboat bed with Captain Ahab. "Queequeg," he said, straightening the sail tied to the curtain rod. "If I've told you once, I've told you a thousand times, no good can come from dancing. Have you ever heard of Isadora Duncan?"

I shook my head.

There was such disappointment in his eyes. "All I can say is avoid wearing long scarves, if at all possible."

The words of a sage. After that, the captain and me sailed quietly in the Caribbean sun. That is, until Nan got home from work to interrupt our solitude. She called me by my people name. Not Queequeg, or Anna Karenina, or one of the other storybook names I was accustomed to using. Some days I swear she didn't even try. But there was something in Nan's tone that made me uneasy. It must have been the way it curled up at the edges before lashing itself to my eardrums. She only said two words. "Celia Canterberry." But in that address, so much more was meant.

"I wasn't arrested," I blurted out, rushing down the stairs. "And Agnes Obermeyer said dancing is not the same as loitering, and there's no bylaw against paying tributes. Besides, she said Archibald might see me and rethink making Eugenia her new best friend."

Nan took a seat at the chrome table. "I'm missing something." She pulled me onto her lap and I started at the beginning. As I spoke, I watched Nan's face. It was like a thermometer. The madder she got, the more the blush rose in her cheeks. She didn't interrupt or ask questions; she was too busy scowling.

"And when we didn't get arrested," I finished, "and Archibald didn't come out, Agnes and me went our separate ways."

"Oh sweetie," Nan said, pulling me closer, her cheek resting on the top of my head. "I'm so sorry. Archibald didn't even notice. Eugenia has her tied up in knots. I don't think she knows whether she's coming or going. *Pick anything you want.*" Nan mimicked Eugenia at the candy counter. "*Except that. And that. You're such a silly girl. I'll do the picking for you.*" I could have slapped her. I tell you Celia, Archibald is disappearing before our eyes, and both her mother and I are at a loss about what to do."

My heart thumped in my chest. Nan had talked to Mrs. Willoughby, and they weren't any happier than I was. I wasn't alone.

"But I don't know if a Lawrence Welk tribute is your best course of action. Then again, I'm glad to hear you're trying."

I brightened. "At recess Timmy Crybaby-Head and me threw dead flies at them."

"Why am I not surprised?"

I smiled at not being reprimanded. Nan, in her own way, was giving me carte blanche.

Nan slipped me off her lap, went to the percolator, and poured herself a cup of coffee. "On the bright side," she said, adding a couple teaspoons of sugar and a splash of cream, "after I served the Whitford's insufferable niece, I went straight to the storeroom. I heard Enid screech Agnes' name, but that's not unusual. It wasn't until I was restocking the magazine rack that I knew things were off. Enid harrumphed back to the residence, banging around. And Fred rubbed his greedy hands together as if he were the cat that swallowed the canary." Nan blew out her cheeks, making her lips flap. "Strangest thing to watch her serve coffee to folks she usually wouldn't give the time of day. Asking if they wanted cream and sugar. I thought she was going to lose her mind when Fred made her go around with a tray of biscuits." Nan chuckled, as if the scene was still alive in her imagination. "Stranger still, I was forbidden to help. Fred said it wasn't my job. Sales were up, and I was needed behind the counter." She tapped me on the top of the head. "And now, Miss Swiss, I know why."

"Did he give you a raise?"

"How did you know?"

I shrugged.

Nan narrowed her eyes before continuing. "Come to think of it, he did ask me the oddest thing. He wants to know when you can come back and perform with your spider web and dust bunny circus."

My jaw dropped. I'd given up on my circus performances after I'd been banned from the drugstore. What's the use of trying to dazzle a crowd that isn't highly medicated? People that are meandering down the street aren't nearly as gullible. Pick the folks loaded up on valium, and the quarters fly. I rubbed my hands, as if preparing to roll an invisible dice. "C'mon, snake eyes! Celia needs a new pair of shoes."

20

When I slipped into my desk the next day, Eugenia, in all her glory, was standing at the front of the classroom basking in the affection of the ludicrous Miss Dobbs. Eugenia had the smuggest look on her face. It made me want to smack her. Archibald, cheeks as hot as firecrackers, as usual, stood two steps behind. Her eyes didn't meet mine, or anyone else's in the room. She just stood there, shuffling a stack of papers and looking pathetic.

"I know it's not our regular show and tell day," Miss Dobbs began. "As you all know, there are no regular show and tell days anymore. Days that featured Eugenia and her amazing collection of toys. Toys she's been forbidden to take to school." She paused for dramatic effect. "As a certain somebody has threatened to dash them to the ground."

I wanted to put up my hand and remind Miss Dobbs that it was one toy, a Chatty Cathy doll to be precise, and I didn't threaten to dash it to the ground. I suggested dropping her down an outhouse or lighting her hair on fire. Chucking her to the ground was only a last resort. But I knew that I would be wasting my breath. Miss Dobbs would believe whatever she wanted.

"Such violence," Miss Dobbs went on, "caused this dear heart no end of grief. And that's why show and tell has been cancelled."

The whole class turned and glared at me. I shrugged.

"Instead, out of the goodness of her heart, Eugenia has another surprise for us." Miss Dobbs brightened.

"Ah, Miss Dobbs," I interrupted, leaning back in my desk, the way anyone who'd been given carte blanche would do. "Is she going to tell us how to steal friends and criticize people? That seems to be her forte." It felt good to strike the first blow. I waited for Eugenia to parry.

Eugenia stiffened, and for a second I thought I had her. That's when I learned that there was no love lost between Eugenia and the French. She didn't parry, let alone respect the unspoken international rules of carte blanche. No. She bulldozed.

"You're so silly," she cooed. "If you'd like, I can talk about what you've been singing in the girl's bathroom. Crybaby-Head and me have heard you halfway down the hall. Haven't we Crybaby-Head?" Her laser-beam gaze almost eviscerated Timmy, before settling on Archibald.

My heart fell into my shoes. What was Archibald to think? That I would croon her life's devastations for all and sundry? That I'd be that heartless? Especially in a room that had the worst acoustics in the whole school? Would she think me a fool? If it weren't against school rules, I'd challenge Eugenia to a hair-pulling contest. When they were girls, Nan and Griggs used to have them. Griggs kept a chunk of Nan's hair in a locket around her neck, to remind her of days when she was victorious.

As a last resort, I called upon Crybaby-Head for support. "Sir Percy," I hissed. "To arms."

He didn't stir. He'd looked into the eyes of a succubus and barely survived. Now he was his old, dehydrated self. I walked to the supply closet for the mop.

"Well." Miss Dobbs tapped her foot. "If Celia is finished taking up everyone's time, we will get back to the matter at hand. Eugenia, take it away."

Eugenia tilted her head and blinked. It was the same look I'd seen her empty-headed cousins use. Except Eugenia wasn't empty-headed. Her head was filled with cruel spite. "As all of you should know by now, my father is a doctor." She looked around the room, as if every time she spoke those words it was an ominous revelation. "And his office is above my uncle's drugstore. Making them the two most important men in town."

I rolled my eyes. Eugenia was doing a book report on herself. The most boring book report ever uttered. I was just about to put up my hand and tell her so when things went south.

"And his window looks down on the street, so he can keep an eye on what's going on. Most days, in a little town like this, there's nothing to see. That is, until yesterday. Yesterday, he had just finished with one of his more annoying patients—I won't name names, but her son is in this class and often smells like pee—when he strolled over to the window. He glanced down and who should he see? Celia Canterberry, that's who. She was loitering outside the drugstore window with someone I'm not allowed to talk to." When no one gasped, she did a little gasp of her own. "Agnes Obermeyer."

I wanted to tell her she had terrible timing. That she should have gasped after she uttered Agnes' name, not before. It was simple stagecraft. But it didn't matter. The way Eugenia said

Agnes' name made the class sit up straighter. She made the pair of us sound as notorious as Bonnie and Clyde.

"The two of them were putting on quite a show. My father was so riveted that he had his nurse cancel his afternoon appointments."

By now the class was hanging on Eugenia's every word. It was like she was Miss Dobbs' junior witch apprentice and had cast them under a spell. I narrowed my eyes and tried to glare her down, but the nasty little thing didn't seem to care.

"Has anyone watched the Lawrence Welk Show?" she went on.

A few kids put up their hands.

"With my grandma," Timmy Crybaby-Head said, as if he were trying to get into the succubus's good books. "She makes me watch it with her every Saturday night. We haven't missed a show in years." He put his head down on his desk, and his shoulders heaved. But I knew he was faking it. Crybaby-Head was a Welkian through and through. I'd heard it in the way he talked to his dead flies, the fake German accent slipping in unaware. "Vonderful, vonderful," he cooed to their lifeless bodies. "If you folks ever have zee pleasure of meeting zis fly in person"—he tried to make the fly take a bow but only managed to rip the thing in two—"I believe you vould find him as delightful as I do." Timmy Crybaby-Head worshipped the man.

"Well anyways," Eugenia droned on, "right under my father's nose, in broad daylight, Celia and Agnes clasped hands and began some kind of tribal dance. Nothing like you'd see on the show. That's when my father got a wonderful idea for a contest. A colouring contest. He thought there was no better way to show off children's creativity than to have them colour their own little town's oddities. And who could be odder than those two?"

"To make a long story short," Miss Dobbs took over, "Dr.

Whitford approached Oswald Elliot, that pencil-necked cartoon sketcher, and told him I'd be ever so grateful if he cobbled something together for my little class; that it might even put him back into my good graces." Miss Dobbs chuckled. "Dr. Whitford has quite a sense of humour." She snapped her fingers and Archibald came to life. She began trudging down each row, handing out mimeographed copies of Oswald's creation.

Sally Shephard put up her hand. "What do we get if we win?"

"Oh, that's the best part." Miss Dobbs beamed. "The winning creation gets featured in this week's Canterberry Tales cartoon strip."

A hum filled the classroom, as kids foraged in their desks for bits of crayons and inhaled the fumes from the mimeographed sheets. I was dumbfounded. How could anyone get involved with a scheme designed by Eugenia Whitford? The girl who wouldn't give the time of day to any of them unless she wanted something. Even Crybaby-Head, seemingly forgetting our recent foray, dug around eagerly in his desk for crayons. I wanted to smack him. And when Archibald, my once-best friend, got around to my desk, she paused. I wanted her to say something—reach out, squeeze my hand, tell me that she too hated Eugenia Whitford and Miss Dobbs was a cow—but she didn't even look at me. Instead, she dropped the sheet on my desk and was gone before the fluttering paper could settle. I felt like the leper in the Bible but couldn't bring myself to utter the words *unclean, unclean*. Eugenia had already done it for me.

As my classmates got to work, I scanned the paper. Griggs would be disappointed. There was no chiaroscuro. The perspective was all off, as if he'd been in a frenzy, dashing off unformed ideas. But no one except me seemed to notice. *You call this art?* I wanted to say, waving the paper in the air. *The man's a hack. Anyone who's ever held a crayon can see that.*

What bothered me most was Oswald Elliot's depiction of me. It was the worst one yet. The whole Lawrence Welk tribute seemed to have gone right over his head. All he'd seen were two semi-professional dancers. My seasonal head didn't resemble Bobby or Sissy. It was some kind of worn out tap shoe. And Agnes hadn't fared any better. She looked like she was related to my should-have-beens, all hunchbacked and snaggle-toothed. Her crinkled cigarette, hardly a stump, ready to glow like a beacon to the den of iniquity. I drew an X through the whole thing before laying my head on my desk to start plotting revenge. Revenge that didn't include the high-minded principles of the French. Revenge that Eugenia couldn't wiggle out of.

21

Doing the supper dishes was more of a rush than usual. Nan didn't allow me to leisurely stir the soap bubbles while we discussed the day's events. Instead, she barked out orders, like, *Celia, quit clowning around,* and *Celia, take the dishtowel off your head.* I wanted to tell her I wasn't having any fun at all, but that would only have given her the impression that I liked chores. Which I didn't. I just disliked these chores less. She didn't settle down until we started popping the corn. "I don't know why I let you talk me into this," Nan said, giving the pot a shake.

I could feel my hackles rise. I hadn't talked her into anything. Griggs had joined our book club when she overheard me talking to Nan about it, and Walter Douglas when he eavesdropped while changing the storm windows. Personally, I didn't invite either of them. It was happenstance. But I couldn't tell Nan that; it would only fall on deaf ears.

Griggs was the first to arrive. She breezed into Nan's kitchen as if she owned the place. "Mind the popcorn," were the first words out of her mouth. "You don't want to burn it like last time."

I looked from Nan to Griggs and rubbed my hands together. We were off to an inauspicious start. The best kind.

"It wasn't burnt, Dorigen."

"I beg to differ. But as I was saying to Mr. Griggs earlier, there's a reason all the old maids aren't limited to the popcorn popper."

The words were barely out of Griggs' mouth when Nan took offence. She slammed the pot down and stepped away from the stove. "If you can do better, have at it."

Old Lady Griggs bristled. "And aggravate my bursitis? Even for you, Molly Canterberry, that's beyond the pale. If I'm not careful, you'll poison my coffee next."

Nan muttered, "Don't think that hasn't crossed my mind," but I'm pretty sure Griggs didn't hear.

As usual, Griggs was oblivious. She waved a hand through the air. "Or plague me with warts, or, let's say borborygmus."

That's when the penny dropped. I looked from Griggs to Nan. Griggs wasn't trying to cause a fight. She was slipping in the dictionary game, trying to catch Nan unaware; get her so riled up she wouldn't know what hit her. If Griggs trounced Nan now, I'm sure she'd refuse to play ever again, claiming that one thorough trouncing was enough in a lifetime, as if her refusal would be doing Nan a favour.

Nan turned back to the stove, pensive. I'd seen that look before. It happened whenever I tried to pull one over on her. Whether Griggs knew it or not, the jig was up. It was all there in the way Nan set her jaw and stiffened her shoulders. I waited, and there it was. The snort. "In your family," Nan let her words fall one by one, "borborygmus is as common as hunger pains."

"Or flatulence," I chimed in.

Griggs was speechless. All her plotting and scheming had been for naught. "I don't want to play anymore," she said. "The two of you are so busy showing off, fawning over the dictionary like a long-lost cousin, it's indecent. So obsessed that you don't even notice when..." She paused as she searched for something we'd neglected to mention. Her lips thinned. "I can't bring myself to say it."

"Well, then I won't have to bring myself to hear it," Nan said.

Griggs had a decision to make. She could either storm out of the house, slamming the door to drive home her point, or she could muster what little grace she had, and take her spot on Nan's chesterfield. The chesterfield was the shorter walk. But she punctuated her displeasure by dropping down so hard on the cushion that the springs groaned in protest.

Nan dumped the popcorn into her large tin mixing bowl before turning to me. "Well done," she said.

I almost purred with pleasure.

Walter Douglas showed up next. He hovered in the doorway, waiting for Nan to formally invite him over the threshold. "Glad you could make it," she said, as she took his coat.

Walter nodded and wiped his shoes on the mat.

"Dorigen is in the living room. You're welcome to join her."

Walter flushed and reached for his coat, but Nan caught his arm before he could retrieve it from the hook. "Or you can join us in the kitchen."

He seemed happy at the prospect and pulled out a chrome chair. We silently busied ourselves with adding tumblers, napkins, and fresh lemonade to one of Nan's best serving trays. I got to carry a plate of chocolate chip cookies to set alongside the bowl of buttered popcorn on Nan's coffee table. Nan was ready to start reading when Agnes Obermeyer strolled in.

"Hope I'm not late," she said. "When Celia told me about your club I just had to come."

Nan glared at me before addressing Agnes. "How did you know it was tonight?"

"I've been camped out in your hedge, and when I saw the others walk in, bold as brass, I knew this was the night."

"You must be freezing," Nan said, taking her coat.

"Not at all. I was sharing a blanket with Oswald Elliot. I even got the bigger half, as long as I let him call me Caroline." She blew on her hands. "That man lacks a lot of things, but dedication isn't one of them."

I thought Nan was going to call off book club then and there, but it wasn't the first time Oswald Elliot had made a home in her hedge, and it probably wouldn't be the last. She seemed resigned to her predicament. Griggs grunted her disapproval from the living room and called out to us in the kitchen. "If I've told that man once, I've told him a thousand times, caraganas are not suitable for inclement weather. 'Build yourself a proper blind,' I said. 'At Molly's age, and with her arthritic neck, she rarely looks up anymore.'"

"You're so helpful, Dorigen," Nan said, entering the living room. There wasn't a bit of gratitude in her voice.

"I do my best."

Nan motioned for all of us to take our places, which created a little kerfuffle. Both Griggs and Agnes wanted to be Nan's bookends, in case there were any pictures—which left me in the cheap seats with Walter Douglas. Nan drummed the cover of *Sense and Sensibility*. "Now where did we leave off?"

I was just about to tell her when Griggs raised her hand. "I believe," she said, smugness dripping from every pore, "that the Dashwoods had been evicted from their residence by an exceedingly selfish brother and gone to live at Barton Cottage. The cottage was owned by Mrs. Dashwood's cousin, Sir John. Shortly after moving to said cottage, Marianne Dashwood and her younger sister Margaret ventured out on a walk, in which Marianne took a tumble."

Nan and I blinked our mutual admiration. It was the one

and only time I thought Griggs sounded refined. Maybe this book was paying off. Griggs had transformed overnight. But then she drew a breath and our illusion was shattered. "And that's when Tiberius, Walter's mangy cat, attacked. He raked his nails down my calf, leaving me scarred for life. I'm lucky I don't have a permanent limp."

Agnes Obermeyer sat up straight in her seat. "So it's an interactive book club? That's so exciting."

"Not on purpose," Nan said through clenched teeth. "But with Dorigen, expect the unexpected."

Griggs smirked while Nan licked a finger. "*Then passing through the garden, the gate of which had been left open by Margaret, he bore her directly into the house, whither Margaret was just arrived, and quitted not his hold till he had seated her in a chair in the parlour.*

"*Elinor and her mother rose up in amazement at their entrance, and while the eyes of both were fixed on him with an evident wonder and a secret admiration which equally sprung from his appearance, he apologized for his intrusion by relating its cause, in a manner so frank and so graceful that his person, which was uncommonly handsome, received additional charms from his voice and expression. Had he been even old, ugly, and vulgar, the gratitude and kindness of Mrs. Dashwood would have been secured by any act of attention to her child; but the influence of youth, beauty, and elegance, gave an interest to the action which came home to her feelings.*"

Nan stopped when Agnes was overcome by tears. "This is Caroline Dobbs and Oswald Elliot all over again," she sobbed. "Once, when I was spying on them from behind some bushes, I saw her drop a pencil. He bent down, without any thought to his perpetually chapped hands, and plucked it out of the dew-soaked grass before laying it tenderly in her palm." Her hands moved slowly as she re-enacted the scene. "It gave me chills."

"That's nothing," Griggs said, not to be outdone. "When Mr.

Griggs gave me my honeymoon hat, I was the talk of the town. He flung it out the window of his dad's old jalopy as he drove past. I'm sure I heard him shout, 'Hope you're happy," as he sped around the corner. That man was always thinking about my wellbeing. That honeymoon hat hit me square in the face, and I knew there and then he wanted to marry me."

The romance was lost on me. By Griggs' way of thinking, anytime a boy threw sand in my eyes it was a declaration of affection. At this rate, I'd end up with more husbands than I had fingers. I needed to clarify things. "The hat Farmer Hempel farted on?"

"Farmer Hempel isn't the only one that's farted on it. It seems to be a fetish with some men."

Nan rubbed her neck for a long time, as if trying to force the words out of her throat, but the words didn't come. Luckily, Agnes Obermeyer had no trouble filling in the silence.

"I suppose," she sniffed, examining her fingernails, "getting pelted in the face with a plastic flower-covered, fart-smelling, chapeau beats being handed a pencil any day of the week."

The sarcasm was lost on Griggs. "Exactly," she said, like the cat that got the cream. "I can't tell you how many heads that hat turned. There wasn't a couple I passed that the wife didn't whisper something to her husband. All pointing and gaping. Let me tell you, I've never in all my years encountered so much jealousy."

"Jealousy?" Agnes asked for clarification.

"To the core."

"And what does this have to do with Marianne falling down a hill?" I asked.

"Don't ask me." Griggs puffed up like a hen on a roost. "Agnes was the one who brought it up."

Before Agnes could respond, Nan cleared her throat and took up from where she left off. "*She thanked him again and again; and, with a sweetness of address which always attended her, invited him to be seated. But this he declined, as he was dirty and wet. Mrs. Dashwood then begged to know to whom she was obliged. His name, he replied, was Willoughby...."*

As Nan read, Griggs and Agnes tried not to glare at one another, not wanting to give the other satisfaction. I counted the steamboats between each stare-off. Griggs was holding strong at five, trying to give an air of indifference. Agnes could barely make it past two, since she was new to the game. If she wasn't careful, Griggs would eat her for lunch. If Nan noticed, she feigned oblivion and kept reading as if all was copacetic; peas in a pod snuggling for warmth. Except nothing could be further from the truth. And by the time Nan got to the last paragraph of chapter fifteen—*This violent oppression of spirits continued the whole evening*—the words were like a self-fulfilling prophecy.

I don't care what anyone says, Gunsmoke has nothing on our book club. The whole thing set my palms to sweating. I was riveted. As Griggs (Festus) and Agnes (Doc) were eyeing each other up, each waiting to out-barb the other, Walter Douglas dozed off, his rough snores supplanting the screech of the Red-Tailed Hawk. Nan, for her part, sat in for Marshall Dillon, keeping the two crones at bay on separate sides of her being. Whereas the real Marshall Dillon prided himself with avoiding female entanglements, Nan had no such qualms. She didn't have to outtalk them or wallop them; Nan out-read them. They couldn't get a word in edgewise. Her voice sped up if either took a particularly unnatural intake of breath, and slowed when they were sizing one another up. All the while, Nan's exuberant tone hammered home the nuances of each page.

"She was without any power, because she was without any desire of command over herself. The slightest mention of anything relative to Willoughby overpowered her in an instant; and though her family

were most anxiously attentive to her comfort, it was impossible for them, if they spoke at all, to keep clear of every subject which her feelings connected with him."

It was book club heaven. But by the time Nan reached the end of the chapter, she was exhausted. Her verbal gymnastics strained her voice and left her bangs stuck to her forehead. She clapped the book shut and motioned to the door. "Can I get your coats?" she asked, without the usual recap.

Griggs and Agnes seemed taken back at her abruptness. "I suppose," said Griggs.

"If you insist," said Agnes.

"I do," Nan said, before covering the distance between the chesterfield and the coat hooks in the porch in record time. "And don't worry about the dishes," Nan said, tossing each of their coats. "Celia and I will be glad to take care of them."

I wanted to protest, saying that dish worrying was the neighbourly thing to do; that women their age should be marked by dishpan hands and worry lines. But Nan must have sensed it coming and shot me a look that made the words wither on my tongue.

Before Agnes scooted out the door, she leaned down and whispered, "Oh, by the by, I've been meaning to tell you. Mr. Murry phoned earlier. I let it ring fifteen times, so you can imagine the importance of the call." She looked so pleased that I was about to tell her she was pretty. "Apparently, business is down and he'd like a little Lawrence Welk sidewalk show. Are you interested?"

I was, but I couldn't tell Agnes Obermeyer until I cleared it with Nan.

Only Walter Douglas remained. Nan tenderly touched his knee to bring him out of his peaceful slumber. "Walter," she said, "it's time to go."

"Did I miss anything?"

"No."

He sniffed before gathering himself. Nan didn't rush him to the door as she had the others; they ambled side-by-side. She held out his coat for him to slide his arms through, and then straightened the collar before slowly opening the screen door. As we watched Walter Douglas being swallowed up by the night, my heart did a little trill.

"I'm not alone," I said. "Not with my very own real-life curiosities."

Nan reached down and squeezed my hand.

22

I stood dumbfounded as Griggs spread the latest edition of the Happy Valley Journal on Nan's chrome table. "Where's your nan?" she whispered.

"Still at work."

"Thank God." Her voice returned to its usual volume. "Some things are best for her to discover on her own. And this," her finger jabbed at the newsprint, "is one of them."

Side by side, Griggs and me did our usual critique. There were four parts to examine, and I didn't like any of them. First was the winner from Dr. Whitford's coloring contest, which could have been predicted before a crayon was pulled from the box. A panel of blind judges meant the judges were blind to every other entry except Eugenia's. Hence, Eugenia won. It was front and center on the page, making it hard to miss.

"How on God's green earth did this ever make it into print?" Griggs slapped the page with the back of her hand. "It's so rudimentary, it hardly bears evaluating. Did she add anything to the piece? No. Did it keep the observer engaged? No. Is it life changing? Clearly not. Frankly Celia, I can't see how she can be the bane to your existence. She hasn't earned it. Squandering an opportunity like this as if it happens every day. Sadly, she's as disappointing as every other Whitford I've met."

Letting out a sigh, I had to admit Griggs was right. As a nemesis, Eugenia relied on the old standbys, like making fun of a kid at recess and whispering their secrets behind their back, but when given the opportunity to excel, crickets. She didn't just colour between the lines, her colour choices were banal, neither brightening the spirit nor pushing one into the depths of despair. How could anyone celebrate that? And that wasn't even considering her lack of add-ons. Where were my devil horns? Neck goiter? Ape-like appendages? Obviously the girl had never seen Griggs' oeuvre.

Griggs pointed to the next section. "Does this look familiar?"

"Partially." It was the extended version of the picture Oswald had drawn for the class. "But this time it was a spate of three boxes side by side. "Still very rudimentary," I said, scanning the additions.

"You're missing the point." Her finger jabbed the page, and that's when I saw her. Milling amongst all the other rubberneckers was my should-have-been ma. Oswald had drawn her as a midnight drooler, but nonetheless, there she was.

"Oswald may be unorthodox, but he is accurate. If he drew her there, she was there."

I sat down in the nearest chair. My should-have-been was so close she could have spit on me. Probably did. The thought gave me the chills.

"You know, that first day I gave you advice on how to make friends, I thought I saw her. She was peeking out from a parked car across the street, but her head was wrapped so tightly with a dingy peacock scarf, I couldn't be sure."

"Did you tell Nan?" My words were so small I wasn't sure if she could hear them.

"Absolutely not. That woman has enough to worry about. I did tell Mr. Griggs though. It's been keeping him up at night. Neither one of us can figure out what that woman is up to. But whatever it is, it isn't good." Once again she stabbed the paper with a jagged nail. "Did you see this?"

I looked to where she was pointing. In the box next to the one my should-have-been was in, were the PIS ladies in all their glory; backcombed hair and starched collars. And the gaggle of them were carrying a sign, *A SOCIETY AGAINST ... WHATEVER THIS IS!* It had a big arrow pointing to Agnes and me.

"Those ladies have too much time on their hands. And that arrow isn't even straight. You'd think at least one of them would own a ruler. Is that too much to ask? But it's this next part that concerns me more than one of your errant should-have-beens and a bunch of busybodies." Griggs cleared her throat and began to read in her Agnes Obermeyer voice.

"Throwing discretion to the wind, two of Happy Valley's more uncivilized citizens cause a near fatal traffic jam. The only thing preventing it is the lack of traffic. Dancing in the most heathenistic manner, they draw a large crowd. Wide-eyed innocence is wiped away by their unnatural gyrations. If it weren't for Mr. Whitford stepping in like the pied piper with offers of beverages and snacks, only God knows what might have transpired."

I had to admit it was mostly right. That's when Griggs pointed to the next box. Agnes Obermeyer and me were walking home, hand in hand.

"That never happened," I said.

"Well, no one in their right mind would think it did. This frame is called a carrier frame, and its job is to bring the story forward. That's why you have three dots for shoes. They're called ellipses."

I was pretty sure she made that word up, but I don't think she cared what I thought, as she'd already moved on to the next frame. It was our book club meeting. Oswald Elliot's bush lurking had paid off in spades. Agnes was sprawled out on Nan's chesterfield, while Griggs picked out the lint from between her toes. Walter Douglas, lost almost entirely inside a pillow fort, and me, with my seasonal head represented by a red checker piece, sat crossed-legged on the floor, playing draughts. All the while, Nan, in an old-fashioned habit, stood at a makeshift pulpit, pontificating on some obscure literary refer-ence. There was neither hide nor hair of any of my storybook friends.

"If you don't consider the subject matter," Griggs started, "I can't help but shake my head. See these lines?" She pointed to the prostrate Agnes. "They're tight, and don't match the flow of her disorganized thoughts."

I nodded. "His heart isn't in it."

"Neither is his brain. He's writing mumbo-jumbo." Griggs began to read. *"On a crispy fall afternoon, an unexpected run-in inspires an unexpected conversation. 'Oh contraire, mon frère,' Mayor Forde says, while moving a toothpick from one side of his mouth to the other. 'I don't think it's a book club at all. It's a ploy to recruit miscreants and malcontents.'*

"'For what purpose?' This intrepid reporter asks, using his best diction.

"'God only knows with that bunch. Tried to lure me in! Me! Just last month, Celia Canterberry herself came to my office and passed me a note.'

When questioned further on the note's content, the mayor refuses to comment. Shaking his head, he says it wasn't fit for man or beast.

And as for this notorious gathering? Meeting in the dead of night, with no sound patriarch to lead the way, and reading God knows what? It's unconscionable. They could be discussing anything. Reading anything. Possibly Mein Kampf *or* The Communist Manifesto*!*

"'If only we could be so lucky,' says Mayor Forde, pacing his office as droplets of sweat do their level best to escape his deeply creased frown lines. 'More likely than not, it's The Feminine Mystique. *Nothing good can come of that. Just ask one of my ex-wives.' He paces the room once more before catching his breath. 'All I can say is, you've got the vote, ladies, now stay home and bake some pies.' As this reporter can attest, it is a sentiment any God-fearing Happy Valleyan would lay claim to."*

But Oswald hadn't stopped there. For the first time in the Happy Valley Journal's history, my comic strip and Archibald's, *A Deadman's Wife*, simultaneously appeared on the same page. It was very much like our book club vignette, the first one the Oswald Elliot pretender had drawn. Just one box, but in it, so much was said. Archibald's mom, Mrs. Willoughby, was sitting at a fancy desk counting bags of money. Snaking away from her was a line of men. I recognized a few of them—Dr. Whitford, Skinny Figgler and of course Oswald Elliot. Underneath it was a one-word caption: *Next.*

I gasped and leaned in closer. Through a smudged window glass over Mrs. Willoughby's shoulder, I could just make out the worried image of Miss Dobbs, peering in and wringing her hands. I almost felt sorry for her, when I knew in my heart I should only be feeling sorry for Mrs. Willoughby. Oswald Elliot had drawn her as if she gloried in the demise of her husbands. Measured them up for their coffins before the wedding ring had a chance to leave a tan line on their finger. It was that thought that brought a tear to my eye. "Poor Archibald."

"Poor Archibald is right. If she was down in the mouth before...." Griggs didn't finish the thought, so I finished it for her.

"She'll be heartsick now."

Griggs gave a curt nod before flipping the page. "Enid Whitford is behind this, attacking on all fronts, and if anyone needs more proof, here it is."

Bold as brass at the top of the fold was Mrs. Whitford's new column. Griggs didn't use her Agnes Obermeyer voice this time; she was too wound up. This time she sounded like pinch-nosed Mrs. Whitford herself.

Titian in Transition
Fair and Honest Reflection

Being the only person with journalistic integrity in our fair town, I've taken it upon myself to interview myself.

Myself: Enid, may I call you Enid?"

Myself: I can't see why not.

Myself: So Enid, when you were first approached by the Happy Valley Journal to be the author of this fine column, did you hesitate? Doubt the accuracy of your immense accumulation of facts?

Myself: Not for a minute. Why would I? I've never been a journalist before, but I have integrity, so I'm halfway there. Even my husband says I never let anything drop, that my mind is like a steel trap. Once an idea takes root, God himself couldn't free me from the notion. I think it's my gift.

Myself: I'm impressed. What can the readership expect in the coming weeks?

Myself: So glad you asked. What this town needs is someone to shake it from its slumber. Open its eyes to the rabble that lies beneath its shabby posterior.

Myself: And you think you are the man to do it?

Myself: Oh don't be silly. I'm not a man, nor would I be so bold as to snatch the opportunity of employment from any hard-working gent who wanted to feed his family by the sweat of his brow.

Myself: I take it when you say employment you are not just talking about writing for the local newspaper?

Myself: Spot on. You are so intuitive. No, I'm talking about jobs like sweeping the street or stalking shelves, like the ones in our very own drugstore.

Myself: I see your point. What kind of woman would want to stalk shelves?

Myself: I ask that question almost every day.

Thank you for reading the reflections of Happy Valley's Number One Titian in Transition.

Griggs snorted, and just like that her regular voice came out. "Enid is right about one thing; she is the biggest TIT in town."

"You have a point there. But what layer of hell will Nan be in when she sees this?"

"Not one I care to witness. I suggest you make yourself scarce until she has time to cool down. I'm heading home."

"To bake pies?" I asked.

"Not in a month of Sundays," Griggs said, before the door shut behind her.

My head thumped on the table. Griggs was right about the Whitfords. I'd been so focused on Eugenia that I'd neglected the swarm of wasps she kept company with. I'd have to widen my net. I banged my head a couple more times. If I was overwhelmed before, I was at my wits' end now.

23

The Halloween Spooktacular wasn't as horrible as I'd imagined. Mostly. Nan had cooled down after she'd crumpled, ripped, and burned the Happy Valley Journal. As an encore, she scorched at least three suppers in a row, causing us to miss the main course and go straight to dessert. That part I really didn't mind.

It was the way she put her lipstick on the night of the Spooktacular that threw me for a loop. She did it over pursed lips, and when she turned to speak to me, her mouth stretched to regular size, making her lips look like a patchwork quilt. But paired with her practical shoes and everyday clothes, it worked. All in all, she looked every bit as good as Sally Shephard's mom, minus the facial hair.

Entering the hall I looked towards the stage. My second grade class was lined up in their Sunday best as Miss Dobbs had instructed. She'd said we were representing her and had to look halfway decent, not like a bunch of clowns. Went so far as to send a note home demanding our clothes be clean, ironed, and if need be patched, with no stains. It landed in the same heap of rubbish as that week's Happy Valley Journal. Nan said it was condescending, and had the smell of a Whitford crony all over it. As if parents needed to be told how to care for their children. She said she was almost of the mind to let me wear a Halloween costume, despite knowing there would be a heavy price to pay.

Leaving Nan's side, I took my place at the back of the line, next to Timmy Crybaby-Head.

He nodded surreptitiously.

"Sir Percy?" I asked, looking to the floor. Not a dribble; he was back.

The two of us stood there, itching and miserable like everybody else, and for once, we both fit in. While the rest of the kids in Happy Valley were out enjoying the real Spooktacular, bobbing for apples, and exploring haunted houses, we were stuck in the hall together. We few; we unhappy few. We band of Unhappy Valleyans.

As the hall filled, it was easy to see the audience was of the same mind, shuffling their feet and grumbling greetings. That is, until Agnes Obermeyer arrived. "I'm here," she announced, pushing her way down the row to get to our book club. Ever since she'd filled in for the school secretary at the Happy Valley School for Reluctant Children, she thought the school revolved around her. She blew kisses and waved at all the kids, reeling off a whole list of names, not one of which matched the kid it was intended for, except me. She got my name bang on. And before she could do anymore damage, Nan took her by the arm and forced her to take a seat.

I looked down their row. Nan, Mr. and Mrs. Griggs, and Agnes were all clumped together. My heart gave a little flutter. No one seemed to want to join them at first, leaving the seats on either side empty. That is, until Farmer Hempel and his wife came in. He seemed delighted that they had saved him a spot, and he announced his appreciation at the top of his lungs. Griggs panicked and tried to hide her honeymoon hat in Nan's purse. Nan snatched her purse away and glared. And with no one minding him, Mr. Griggs slid to the floor, his cotton-stuffed head lolling to one side.

It made me kind of sad inside that they didn't need me to cause a scene. Still, I felt so proud, I was sure I'd burst. They were all mine.

Mrs. Willoughby strolled in next, head held high, as if Oswald Elliot's unkind words and pictures hadn't touched her; couldn't touch her. Her brood were no different. They followed her down Nan's row like a bunch of illiterate ducklings, oblivious to any snickering. Heads held every bit as high as their mother's and smiling to beat the band. Even Grenway, with his marvellous cheek dimples, was there. And from where I stood, those dimples looked as lovely as ever, not all stretched out and saggy from Eugenia's pudgy fingers poking. Only Walter Douglas stood off by himself. He waited next to the door, one hand on the handle for a quick escape.

It was time for Miss Dobbs' big moment. Looking directly at Dr. Whitford, and ignoring the rest of us, she called Archibald and Eugenia to the stage. There was no arm swinging or whispered giggling. In fact, Archibald stomped her way to the front of the stage, arms crossed in front of her as if daring anyone to ask her to smile. Eugenia didn't even notice. She was too busy waving and blowing kisses into the crowd.

Miss Dobbs cleared her throat. "Ladies and gentlemen, may I have your attention? This year's committee for the Halloween Spooktacular, The Ladies of the Perpetual Indigence Society, have graciously asked my humble class to be the headliners. Over the next hour we will do just that. We will offer presentations on the esteemed members of our neighbourhood, and our community. And let me tell you, it's been more than a delight. The privilege of working with this exceptional group gets me up in the morning. And by exceptional, I mean Eugenia Whitford."

Eugenia curtsied.

"How one student can tip the balance boggles the mind, but she has. She brightened the class as soon as she stepped through the door. And that's why Eugenia's leading the way. Eugenia and her little sidekick." Miss Dobbs looked at Archibald with a blank expression.

Archibald's eyes narrowed as she mouthed, "Archibald Quigley."

"That's right. Archibald Quigley! How could I forget the little fatherless girl?" She leaned over and tweaked Archibald's cheek. "Anyway, Eugenia is going to entertain us with the people in her neighbourhood." She stepped aside with a flourish. "Take it away, Eugenia."

That's when I mostly zoned out. Going over what Eugenia said would only bore me for a second time. In a nutshell, she droned on and on about her father, comparing him to the famous Greek physician, Hippocrates. She said that if it weren't for Hippocrates, the Hippocratic Oath would be attributed to her father, and it would be called the Whitfordcratic Oath. At that point, Archibald was supposed to jump up and down with glee. She did the jumping, but I didn't see much glee. In fact, she looked miffed playing second fiddle.

Nan rolled her eyes and elbowed Griggs. "Whitfordcratic oath, my Aunt Fanny."

"I think you mean Celia's Aunt Fanny," Griggs corrected. "That woman's not related to you. At your age, you should understand that."

Nan's voice sharpened, so that even her whisper could pierce eardrums. "Oh, I understand all right."

"I beg to differ. Case in point, you just called her *your* Aunt Fanny."

Nan elbowed Griggs even harder.

I could always count on those two.

But Eugenia wasn't done. When she talked about her uncle the pharmacist, she slapped a Band-Aid on Archibald's forehead a bit too hard, almost knocking Archibald to the floor. She explained her uncle and aunt not only owned a drugstore, but out of the kindness of their hearts employed the less fortunate, though the local paper warned against it. All the PIS ladies turned and stared at Nan. I blinked back tears for her.

"And don't get me started on Miss Dobbs," Eugenia droned on. "She makes the most fantastic muffins. They make me want to be a teacher. Best of all, I'm the apple of her eye." Eugenia did a batty-eyed Shirley-Temple-face pose, while behind her, Archibald abandoned the strip and mimed sticking her finger down her throat.

I'd never loved her more than in that moment.

After Eugenia used up half the entire presentation time, the rest of the kids went through their neighbourhood people with remarkable speed. They were helped along by Miss Dobbs taking out her stopwatch and loud-whispering, *faster, faster*. So much, that it was hard to catch what everyone was saying. I wasn't sure what one of the unremarkable Bobbsey Twins said Farmer Hempel loved more—tractors or his wife. Like it was some kind of contest. Or if Sally Shephard said she was actually allowed to squish Mrs. Jasmine's buns at Saggy Buns Bakery. If it was how it sounded, Mrs. Jasmine was rather forward for an older woman. I wondered if I should introduce her to Captain Ahab.

As the presentations wrapped up, so did the time. Miss Dobbs clip-clopped back on stage. "Sad to say," she chirped, "but we have run out of time, and our last, poorly-prepared group will be unable to present their drivel."

Some of the crowd shifted in their seats, preparing to leave. But then from the back of the room someone started to chant. It was Mayor Forde. I'm not sure why he was there, unless he couldn't let a plum opportunity for Oswald Elliot to sketch his life's ambition go to waste. The chant was low at first, hard to make out, but soon others joined in, and it became a roar. "Seasonal-Head, Seasonal-Head."

I took a deep breath and puffed out my chest. They were chanting my nom de plume! I knew Nan wouldn't be impressed, but Griggs was yowling with the rest of them. Sir Percy turned to me, and I brushed the side of my nose with a tip of a finger. Together we strode to centre stage with a swagger that left Miss Dobbs flummoxed.

He was the Scarlet Pimpernel and I was Boudicca. Together we were going to put on the best 'people in your neighbourhood' show the people in our neighbourhood had ever seen. I had practiced in front of Captain Ahab and whispered it through a crack in the cellar door to Anna Karenina. When both of them seemed unimpressed, I let Griggs and Agnes Obermeyer put their two cents in. Of course, I waited until Nan slipped into the bathroom during book club.

"Does your grandmother know about this?" Griggs had asked, looking over the crumpled piece of paper I pulled from my pocket.

"It's going to be a surprise."

She took a deep breath. "You're right about that. I don't know where to start."

"How about here?" Agnes Obermeyer peered over Griggs' shoulder. "I'd put in, 'A pinch of Fanny Figgler hate.'"

"That works." Griggs had paused and listened for Nan before adding, "I'd slip in 'Whitford' right after 'eye,' here on the third line."

I'd jotted both ideas down. "How about Dobbs?"

"She'd fit in right here." Griggs jabbed at my paper.

Walter Douglas had snuck up on us unaware, and with the

weariest voice he said, "Embers. Sitting in embers. Sitting and waiting."

I didn't even know where to put that. None of us did. Sometimes that man lived in a world of his own. We continued whispering and fussing until Nan flushed the toilet—the signal to slip back to our spots. "Good thing your nan has borborygmus," Griggs had muttered as she settled in, "or we'd have never gotten through your so-called surprise."

Agnes' concern was palpable. "What's borborygmus? And more importantly, will it affect her reading?"

"Her reading, no," Griggs had said, "but you might have to hold your breath while listening."

But even with their help my project still wasn't quite right. I'd fussed with it while Timmy reassembled his flies. I'd fussed while mopping up after him. I'd even fussed while licking up the cupcake crumbs Eugenia shed on my desktop when skipping past. In the end, I'd had no choice. I'd turned to Nan.

"What's a good word for special?"

"You should know that, Celia. We've been playing the dictionary game as long as you've been able to talk."

I shrugged. "But it's not a regular kind of special; it's a special kind of special."

"What kind of special?"

"The kind"—I'd picked my words carefully—"for someone who lives under your heart."

"That's easy. Beloved."

"What about an evil magical guy?"

"How about a warlock?"

"Nope."

"A cyclops?"

I shook my head.

"What about a sprite? They're mischievous but often tiptoe into the dark side."

"Maybe," I'd said, as I repeated the word to myself.

Now, with my best side facing the audience so Oswald Elliot could get a really good sketch, I cleared my throat. "Ladies and Gentlemen, I agree with Miss Dobbs. Most everything she teaches us is drivel."

"So instead," Sir Percy said, in a more dignified manner than Crybaby-Head could ever muster, "we're going to recite a poem."

In unison, we both cleared our throats. Spotlights popped up on either side of us, so we were a team standing in each other's shadows. Nothing like Eugenia and Archibald. Sir Percy was not my lackey, and I certainly wasn't going to be his. (Me, a lackey! The thought was ludicrous. Even Sir Percy would say so. Sir Percy, on the other hand, was an aristocrat, and some of them could barely keep their heads.)

Our lungs were filled with air when Griggs chose to come unglued—probably from waiting on pins and needles for us to bring her suggestions to life. She clutched Mr. Griggs' hand to her heart and yelled, "You can do this, Celia. Remember Syphilis!"

That was the most uncomfortable part of the evening. Mayor Forde turned red as if he felt guilty about something, and Nan choked on a breath mint she'd been sucking. Griggs pounded her on the back while she struggled to explain how her syphilis comment was meant to encourage, no matter how dirty minds tried to twist it.

"No one is twisting anything." Nan's voice and coughs rose over the silence.

I ignored them both and soldiered on. First, we set the scene by making groans that took on the sound of a cold night wind, swooping around the hall like winged beasts. Then we hunched our backs over an invisible black cauldron. Our arms strained as we dredged the unseen long-handled spoon through the gurgling brew. And then together we began to recite.

The Midnight Hag (by William Shakespeare, and some lesser talented people).

Double, double toil and trouble;
Fire burn and cauldron bubble.
A pinch of Fanny Figgler hate,
In the cauldron boil and bake;
Eye of Whitford; toe of Dobbs,
Will birth a sprite announced by sobs.
Dragging a Chatty Cathy doll
To the washroom down the hall
With unhinged jaw she'll mock and sing,
And crush our most beloved thing.
No better Helen, our dearest friend
Let's rescue earthworms; make amends.

Sir Percy and me shuddered a breath before we both turned and stared at Archibald.

Now in embers, sit and wait
For our beloved to 'scape her fate
Outrun the clutches of teacher's pet
Most insufferable person we've ever met.
Double, double toil and trouble;
Fire burn and cauldron bubble.

After an uncomfortable silence, Farmer Hempel slapped his knee. "I told you there was something wrong with that kid. Any kid that can unhinge their jaw is one to steer clear of."

His wife elbowed him in the ribs while stifling a grin. I didn't dare look at Nan; wasn't sure there would be any joy in Mudville. That's when Miss Dobbs clip-clopped across the stage, her yardstick slapping her palm. "I want everyone to know that I didn't authorize this. Any of it!" She grabbed me by the ear and gave me a shake. "It was all Audrey's doing."

"I'm not Audrey."

"You're worse," she hissed, loud enough for everyone to hear.

The crowd sat on the edge of their seats, not sure if this was part of the program, or if we were just improvising. That's when the most unexpected thing happened. Archibald Quigley, my once, and now again, best friend, stepped away from the rest of the second grade class, looked Miss Dobbs straight in the eye, adjusted her bolty neck, and let loose her draggy leg. That girl Frankenstein-walked across the stage, down the steps, and out the hall's main door. Everyone stared. Before I could catch my breath at the wonder of it all, brave Sir Percy, dear Sir Percy, sweet Sir Percy, adjusted his own bolty neck and shambled after her.

After that it was mayhem, with Mrs. Willoughby and her brood, Agnes, and the Hempels following Archibald's lead. Griggs brought up the rear, drooling and dragging her husband behind her. All the people that counted in my life were Franken-stein-walking. All except Nan. She was headed straight for Miss Dobbs, with murder in her eyes. And when Nan was done with Miss Dobbs, Dr. Whitford took over. I don't know what he said, but whatever it was, it even made Nan flinch. To this day, it's known as the best Halloween Spooktacular ever.

Celia Should-have-been

1. ~~Get Nan's house back~~
2. ~~Get a new best Friend~~
3. What's a lawyer?

24

That night, when I snuggled between my cool sheets, I felt like Eliza Doolittle from *My Fair Lady*. I could have Frankenstein-walked all night! Not happily, but I could have done it. In fact, I Frankenstein-walked all the way home. My draggy leg cramped so much that I wanted to beg Nan to put me out of my misery. But my pleas would have fallen on deaf ears. Not only because Nan found Frankenstein-walking foolhardy and beneath her dignity, but because Archibald was galumphing along beside me, as if there were no better form of transportation. And if it was good enough for Archibald, it was goddamn well good enough for me.

Apparently, when Sir Percy and me were glorying in our triumphant presentation, bowing to the audience even after the hall had emptied, Nan had gone straight from scolding Miss Dobbs to talking to Mrs. Willoughby. The two of them, Nan and Mrs. Willoughby that is, figured a sleepover was in order. They said it would give Archibald and me time to reconnect.

As I drooled my way home, I could feel my cup running over. Not only did I have my best friend back, I had a handful to spare. Old Lady Griggs, Agnes Obermeyer, Farmer Hempel, and Walter Douglas, to name a few. And Samwise Gamgee. People that loved me all along, despite my should-have-beens. Except Timmy Crybaby-Head, he didn't love me. Said so himself. He only had eyes for Archibald. What a relief!

After Nan gave us cookies and milk, Archibald crawled into bed beside me. "Celia," she said, propping her head up on her bent arm. "Even when I was ignoring you, you were still my best friend."

"Didn't feel like it."

"Occam's razor," she yawned.

Those were my words, the ones I used to irritate Miss Dobbs and baffle Griggs, and they were coming out of Archibald's mouth. I couldn't have loved her more. "I stopped using that particular phrase when you linked arms with Eugenia. That's when my whole world stopped making sense, and if my world didn't make sense there was no room for Occam's razor."

"I know," Archibald said, gently grinning in the moonlight. "But Eugenia told me I needed to protect my mom. That the only reason Oswald Elliot wrote The Dead Man's Wife was because I was your best friend. She said he wouldn't have even noticed our family if it weren't for you. That he had to lump the good—me—with the bad—you. Her Aunt agreed, and she's a drugstore owner's wife. When we were getting candy from the candy counter, Mrs. Whitford said if I was going to lay down with dogs, I shouldn't be surprised if I get up with fleas."

I was a little shocked by the attack. Besides not all dogs having fleas, this week's Happy Valley Journal had published our columns side by side. "But that's not true," I said.

"I know that now."

She reached over and found my hand in the dark. We did an arm swing under the covers.

"Want to see something?" I asked, thinking my magnificent headboard etchings would help solidify our renewed affections.

Archibald nodded.

Letting go of her hand, I slipped my hand under my pillow, retrieved my flashlight, and clicked it on. The beam revealed my list of jaggedly scratched words.

Archibald ran her fingers over the marks and whistled. "Your Nan let you do this?"

"No. It was..."

"The influence of witches," Archibald interrupted.

"Exactly." I knew she'd understand. Archibald was the only one that took my witch talk seriously.

We read through the list together.

1. *Get Nan's house back.* (That was already crossed off.)
2. *Get a new best friend.*

Even in the dark I could tell Archibald didn't like number 2. Her sniffle was more than a sniffle. I reached under my pillow, found my pencil, and handed it to Archibald. "You can cross that one off."

"Will your nan get mad? Like when I tried to harpoon her?"

"It's hard to tell with that woman. Besides, my headboard is already so scarred I don't think she'll notice." I put my hand over hers and we crossed it out together.

"What are you going to do now?" Archibald asked.

I shrugged. Should I find out about the Luger Fanny Figgler talked about? Or wheedle out what that grimy note said—the one my should-have-been pa made me give Mayor Forde? Or perhaps I should thwart Skinny Figgler and save Archibald's mom from a dismal future, even if I was pretty sure she didn't want him in the first place. I turned to Archibald. "What would you do?"

She pointed to number 3. "What's a Luger?"

"Don't know," I said, growing excited, "but it's time *we* found out."

ABOUT THE ILLUSTRATOR

Michelle has always had a love for horses and animals that has influenced her artwork since she could first hold a pencil. She first discovered digital art in 2007 and has never looked back since.

She grew up in Brooks, Alberta, and has attended schools in Vancouver, California and Montreal where she has learned how to cultivate her creativity and improve both herself and her craft.

In addition to animals and creatures, she is also inspired by movies, video games and fantasy fiction. She is excited to someday start an independent project where she can illustrate and write full-time.

To see more of her artwork visit www.michellefroese.com

HELLO MY WONDERFUL
READER,

Thanks for reading *Midnight Hags*. If you enjoyed your time with Celia, a review would be much appreciated as it helps other readers discover the story.

If you have a minute sign up for my intrepid newsletter. Each month, I herald one of my beloved words or turns of phrase, and in turn, you are invited to herald right back. And if your phrase or word is not one I've considered, or one that someone else has suggested, it may end up in my next work of fiction (with an acknowledgement of its sender tucked firmly within the yarn's pages).

I look forward to hearing from you. Thanks again.

All my best,

C.P. Hoff

Join my email list:

www.cphoff.com

CONTENTS